THE BEST OF

WOOF

Danae Dobson

Tyndale House Publishers, Inc.
Wheaton, Illinois

Visit Tyndale's exciting Web site at www.tyndale.com

Illustrations for *Woof Finds a Family, Woof Goes to School, Woof and the Haunted House, Woof and the Midnight Prowler, Woof and the New Neighbors,* and *Woof's Bad Day* copyright © 1989 by Dee deRosa. All rights reserved.

Cover and interior illustrations for *Woof and the Big Fire* and *Woof, the Seeing Eye Dog* copyright © 1990 by Karen Loccisano.

Edited by Betty Free

Cover designed by Julie Chen

The Adventures of Woof were originally published in ten volumes by Nelson-Word, Nashville, TN.

Verses on pages 26, 29, 89, 91, 187, and 251 are taken from the *Holy Bible,* New Living Translation, copyright © 1996. Used by permission of Tyndale House Publishers, Inc., Wheaton, Illinois 60189. All rights reserved.

Verses on pages 61, 123, 153, 155, 181, 183, and 219 are taken from the *Holy Bible,* New International Version®. NIV®. Copyright © 1973, 1978, 1984 by International Bible Society. Used by permission of Zondervan Publishing House. All rights reserved.

Library of Congress Cataloging-in-Publication Data

Dobson, Danae.
   The best of Woof / Danae Dobson.
     p. cm.
   Combines eight of ten previously separately published volumes. Summary: The Peterson children's adventures with their dog Woof teach them about God.
   ISBN 0-8423-0058-9 (hc)
   [1. Dogs—Fiction. 2. Christian life—fiction.] I. Title.
   PZ7.D6614Be 1999
   [E]—dc21   98-53874

Printed in the United States of America

05   04   03
7   6

TABLE OF CONTENTS

INTRODUCTION

You're about to read some fun adventure stories about a mutt named Woof. As you will soon find out, Woof is far from ordinary! For one thing, he's kind of ugly. With his bent ear and tail, and crooked leg, he's not the type of dog most people want for a pet. But Woof is also very brave and smart. And most important, he has a heart filled with love for the family he lives with.

As you read these stories about Woof, I hope you will remember how special *you* are! The Lord made you unique—you're different from everyone else, and God has a definite plan just for you. It doesn't matter how you look or what brand of clothing you wear. What's most important is what's in your heart.

So sit back and enjoy the many adventures of Woof. I'm sure you'll agree he's one lovable mutt!

Danae Dobson

WOOF

FINDS

A FAMILY

THEME

God answers prayer.

Philippians 4:6

It was a wet August day as Krissy and Mark Peterson looked out of Krissy's bedroom window.

"Look how hard it's raining," Mark said, peering down at the sidewalk. "What a day to splash in the puddles!"

"Not now," Krissy replied. "I don't feel like it. Actually, I don't feel like doing anything."

"Me neither," Mark said, looking up at his ten-year-old sister. "Let's just watch the rain."

As they sat by the window, a man in a black raincoat walked briskly down the sidewalk. Stumbling up to him came a wet, shaggy-haired dog that probably hadn't had a bath in weeks. He rubbed his head against the man's pant leg, as if asking to be petted.

"Get away, mutt!" the man shouted and kicked the poor dog into the gutter. "Leave me alone!" The dog lifted his head and watched the man walk down Maple Street.

"Krissy!" Mark said, grabbing her sleeve. "Did you see that?"

Instead of answering, Krissy ran downstairs and out the door. She picked up the dog affectionately, although he was almost too heavy for her to carry. The dog licked her hand gratefully. By the time Mark burst through the front door, Krissy was returning to the house.

"Let me hold him! Let me pet him!" Mark begged impatiently.

"Wait," Krissy replied, frowning at him.

Their mother heard the commotion and came outside, holding a newspaper to shield her hair from the rain.

"Krissy, Mark!" she shouted. "What on earth are you doing with that ugly, filthy dog?"

"Mom, this is our new pup," said Mark. "You can tell he doesn't belong to anyone because he doesn't have a collar. May we keep him?"

"Certainly not. I don't even want to discuss it. Now put him down, and come into the house. Your clothes are soaked already."

But the children would not give up that easily.

"Mom," Mark said. "He doesn't have a home. Couldn't we keep him until tomorrow? *Please?*"

Mrs. Peterson looked at the wet dog. Indeed he was a sight. He looked up at her with pitiful eyes and wagged his crooked little tail. Mrs. Peterson's heart softened as she said, "OK. You may keep him until this weekend—maybe we can find a good home for him by then. He does need a dry bed and some food."

"Oh boy!" both children shouted at the same time. Krissy
put the dog down, and she and Mark began racing toward the
house with the animal beside them.

"Krissy," said Mrs. Peterson, "I don't want to be unkind,
but I refuse to have that filthy dog in our house. You can
make him a bed in the garage and give him a bath."

"All right. Come on, Mark," said Krissy. "You go get a tub
and some soap, and I'll get some old rags and towels."

When the children had everything ready, they set the dog in the tub of soapy water. They couldn't believe how dirty he was. At least a thousand fleas were scampering around his furry body.

"That's why he scratches all the time," said Krissy. "This poor dog must be miserable."

They scrubbed him until he was clean.

"Phew!" Krissy said, wiping the sweat off her forehead. "That's done."

They dried him off and dusted him with flea powder left over from the time they had taken care of the Smiths' cat. Mark found one of his old toothbrushes and brushed the dog's teeth, although the animal didn't seem to appreciate the favor.

"Have you thought about what we're going to name him?" asked Krissy.

"He looks like a Rover to me," said Mark.

"That's too common," Krissy replied. "How about Penny?"

"No-o-o. . . . Hey! Let's ask *him* what he wants to be called," Mark said.

They both looked at the dog. As if he had read their minds, the dog barked. *Woof!*

"How about that?" said Krissy. "He answered us. I think Woof is a great name."

"Me too," Mark said. "Let's name him Woof."

At dinner that evening the children told
their father everything that had happened that
day. They were still upset about the man in the
raincoat, who had kicked their pup.

As Mother was bringing in the dessert, an
awful thing happened. Woof managed to push open the door
between the house and the garage. He bounded into the
kitchen toward his new friends. But as he was coming
through the doorway, he slid on the hardwood floors and
crashed into a tea table that held a beautiful vase. The vase
toppled and fell to the floor, breaking into a million pieces.
Mother shrieked and Father gasped.

Mrs. Peterson began to cry because the vase had been in the family for ninety years. Krissy ran to Woof and started to lead him back to the garage.

"Just look at that mess!" Mr. Peterson said. "Either you find a home for that animal by tomorrow afternoon or he is going to the pound!"

"No," Mark begged. "Please!"

But Mr. Peterson had made up his mind. The two children ran up the stairs in tears. They both knew what the pound usually meant—*Death!*

That night when their father came upstairs to tell the children good night, he found them saying their prayers. They were asking God to help them find a home for Woof so he wouldn't have to go to the pound.

When they finished, they looked up to see their father standing over them. He put loving arms around his children and pulled them close to him.

"You know," he began, in his quiet, steady voice, "I once had an experience like this. We had a dog named Pal when I was a boy, and we had to give him away because we moved. I was sick about losing him, but I soon got over it. That's how it will be with you, too."

"But, Dad, your dog didn't have to go to the pound, did he?" asked Krissy.

"Well, no, we gave him to the people next door. But I don't know anyone in this neighborhood who wants a dog. Besides, this is the ugliest mutt I've ever seen. He has a crooked leg and one ear that flops over. He's just not the kind of dog that people want for a pet."

Mark wiped a tear from his eye.

"Look, if you really want a dog that much, I'll get you a German shepherd puppy," said Mr. Peterson. "He'll be a purebred you can be proud of. OK?"

Krissy broke into tears. "But Woof needs us—he has no family!"

"Don't worry about it anymore," Mr. Peterson said. "You'll feel better in the morning after you've had some rest." He tucked Mark and Krissy into their beds, gave them each a kiss, and went downstairs.

Krissy drifted off to sleep in a matter of minutes, but she soon awoke from a nightmare. She lay there tossing and turning for almost an hour. Finally she got up and slipped downstairs. All was quiet and dark. She thought she saw a figure floating near the wall, but it was only her shadow.

Krissy felt her way into the gloomy garage and looked around. Then she heard a soft patter of feet coming toward her. It was Woof. She knelt beside him and stroked his rough fur. He snuggled up to his new friend and licked her hand as if to say, "I know I'm not worth much. I know I'm ugly and I'm just a mutt. You did what you could, and I understand."

   Krissy couldn't bear it any longer. She gave Woof a last pat
and went back to bed.
   The next morning at breakfast no one talked about the dog.
But everybody was thinking about him. The children picked
at their food while their father tried to get them to think
about other things.

After breakfast Mr. Peterson picked up his briefcase and gave Mother a kiss. As he was nearing the doorway, he turned toward the children. "I'll be home at six o'clock to take care of the dog," he said. Then, seeing the sad look on their faces, he paused and took a deep breath.

"Don't worry, kids," he said. "It's going to be all right." Then he left.

Mrs. Peterson asked the children to do some household chores. Mark finished first, so he went outside and called Woof.

"Come on, boy," Mark said. "Let's see if we can find you a home."

He put Woof in a wagon and pulled him to the McCurrys' house. Then he rang the doorbell.

"Hello," Mark said to Mrs. McCurry. "We're trying to give this dog away. Would you like to have him?"

"I'm afraid not. You see, we already have a dog and two cats. Besides, even if we were getting a dog, I wouldn't want *that* one." She rolled her eyes and shut the door. Mrs. McCurry always was a blunt person.

I guess we're out of luck there. How about the Gossets? Mark thought to himself. The radio was blaring loudly, and Mr. Gosset was outside washing his car.

"Hello," he said. "What can I do for you?"

"Oh, I'm trying to give away this dog," Mark answered. "He doesn't have a home, and we don't want him to go to the pound. Would you take him?"

Mr. Gosset looked down at the ugly mutt and slowly shook his head from side to side. "No, thanks," he said as he continued with his work.

Mrs. Perry was weeding her garden. "Excuse me," Mark said. "Are you interested in having a dog?"

"Did you say dog?" She gave a shrill whistle, and seven puppies came bounding into the front yard.

"I'd best be going," Mark said.

He found his pals playing baseball in the vacant lot near his house.

"Come on, Mark," one of them shouted. "You can be pitcher."

"No, thanks," Mark said. "I'll just watch."

He sat down on the curb, but his mind wasn't on the game. He was thinking about Woof. His thoughts were interrupted when Barney hit a fly ball that bounced on the sidewalk and rolled into the middle of the street.

"I'll get it," Mark said, running toward the ball. But he did not see the minivan that came whizzing around the corner. The driver slammed on the brakes, but it was too late to stop. Mark screamed as the van skidded in the direction of the frightened boy.

Seeing the danger, Woof made a dash for Mark and knocked him out of the way. But Woof didn't have enough

time to save himself. The van hit the back part of his body,
and he skidded across the street, landing in the gutter.

Krissy and Mother heard the commotion and came running
outside. Mark stumbled toward Woof. His tears fell on the
street as he bent over the unconscious dog. Krissy ran back
into the house to get an old blanket, and they wrapped it
carefully around Woof's body. A neighbor carried him to the
Petersons' porch and tried to keep him warm.

Mrs. Peterson hurriedly telephoned her husband to explain what had happened. He arrived home and put Woof in the backseat of the car. The family drove in silence to the Small Animal Hospital.

When they got there, the veterinarian took Woof into the operating room. Before closing the door, he said to Krissy and Mark, "I'll do my best."

The two children nodded appreciatively, but they were worried. Outside, a storm was gathering. The thunder sounded like an echo of what was taking place inside Krissy's and Mark's pounding hearts. Their tears joined with the rain that had begun to fall.

Several hours passed as they sat facing the big white door, waiting and waiting. Krissy turned to her brother. "Maybe we should pray," she said.

They both closed
their eyes and asked
Jesus not to let the dog
die. The big clock on the wall struck eight o'clock.

Finally the vet returned. "Well, your dog has a
broken leg and some internal injuries," he said. "The damage
is not serious enough to take his life, but I really believe Woof
is dying. It's almost as if he doesn't want to live."

Krissy spoke up. "I know what's wrong. Woof doesn't feel
loved. A dog needs love, just like people do."

"You're right about that," said the vet.

"Can we see him?" asked Mark.

"Yes, of course," said the doctor. "Come in."

23

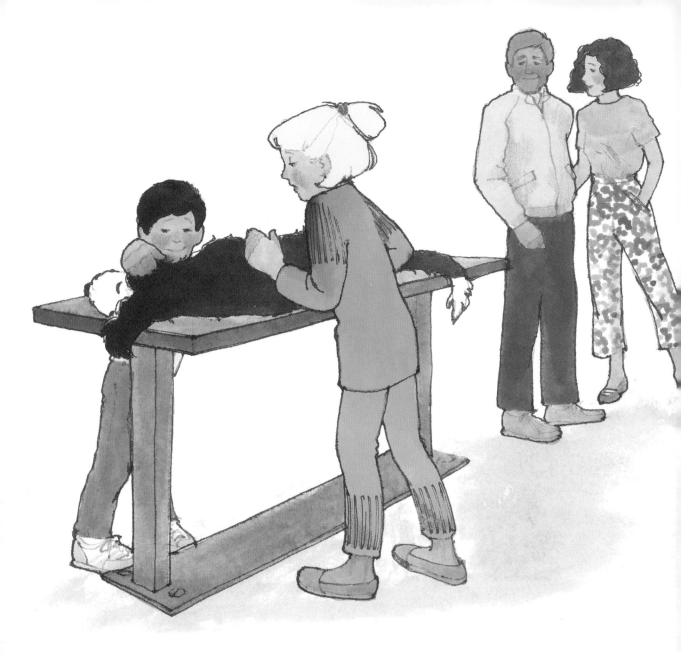

They entered a small room where Woof lay on the table. He
was whimpering softly. Krissy and Mark rushed to him. They
gave him gentle hugs and stroked his rough fur. Mark turned
to his parents, who were watching their children lovingly.

"Krissy is right," he said. "Woof doesn't want to get well,
Dad. He must know he has no place to go. Maybe he
understands he will be taken to the pound if he lives."

The corners of Mr. Peterson's mouth turned upward into
a slight smile.

24

"How could I send a dog to the pound after he saved the life of my son? No sir! If this mutt lives, he is our dog for the rest of his life."

Krissy and Mark squealed with delight. Could it really be true? They laughed and jumped, thanking their mother and father. No one knew if Woof understood why they were so happy, but his little tail wagged just a bit as he rolled his big brown eyes toward them.

"Oh, Woof!" said Krissy. "You just *have* to get well!"

"Let's go home and get some rest now," their father laughed. "Or else we'll be spending time in a people hospital."

The next morning the Petersons received a call from the vet. The children listened closely as their mother talked. After a short conversation, Mrs. Peterson hung up. Her face glowed as she said, "Woof is much better. We should be able to bring him home tomorrow."

The children had never been so excited. "Wait," Mrs. Peterson said firmly. "Didn't you ask God for something?" She then quoted a verse of Scripture from memory: "Don't worry about anything; instead, pray about everything. Tell God what you need, and thank him for all he has done."

Krissy and Mark knelt down by the sofa and thanked the Lord for saving their dog. It really was a miracle!

The next afternoon when Mr. Peterson came home from work, the family went to the Small Animal Hospital again. Woof seemed very happy to see them. He was sore and had a cast on his hind leg, but his tail was not injured. It thrashed back and forth vigorously.

That evening Woof was lying on his blanket while Mark and Krissy helped Mother with dinner. Mark leaned down to give Woof a doggie treat. Neither of the children thought to ask why their father was in the garage or what was causing all the noise.

After supper Mr. Peterson picked up Woof and asked his
family to come outside. There stood a beautiful redwood
doghouse. Above the door was a little sign that read
WOOF
OUR SPECIAL HERO

WOOF FINDS A FAMILY
Theme: God answers prayer.

Talking about Woof

At the beginning of the story, Mark and Krissy's parents didn't want to keep Woof. Why not?

What did Woof do to change their minds?

Talking about Mark and Krissy

Name two times when Mark and Krissy prayed for Woof. What did they ask God to do?

Did he answer their prayers? How?

Talking about Me

Think about some of your prayer requests. What kinds of things have you asked God to do for you?

Which prayers did he answer by saying

    yes?
    no?
    wait?

Reading What the Bible Says

Don't worry about anything; instead, pray about everything. Tell God what you need, and thank him for all he has done. *Philippians 4:6*

Talking to God

Dear God, thank you for listening to my prayers and caring about all the things I need. Teach me to pray when I need something instead of worrying about it. And don't let me forget to thank you for your answer, whatever it is.

    I want to pray for . . .
    Thank you for . . .
    I love you, God. In Jesus' name. Amen.

WOOF

GOES
TO SCHOOL

THEME

God loves everyone, so we
should love each other.

John 3:16

It was the end of an enjoyable summer. A new school year was starting, and all the children in the city of Gladstone were returning to the classroom. Already the first golden autumn leaves had begun to sprinkle the sidewalks along Maple Street.

On the first morning of school, Mark and Krissy Peterson hurried around their rooms, putting on socks and shoes and gathering their book bags. Woof, their dog, sat in the background, watching as they got ready. He understood the

excitement because he had seen children go to school before.
But he was unhappy that Mark and Krissy were leaving.
Woof had been having so much fun since he came to live
with them.

After they finished eating breakfast, the children said
good-bye to their mother and father. They both gave Woof a
pat on the head as they headed for the driveway. Woof stood
whimpering by the front door. He watched Mark and Krissy
round the corner, never taking his eyes off them for a second!
Finally it became too hard to stay put. Woof ran to catch up
with his young friends.

When Mark and Krissy saw him coming, they scolded him for following them. "Woof, you can't come to school with us. Now go home!" Krissy said.

Woof stood with his crooked tail wagging and his tongue hanging out.

"Go on, boy. Go home!" Mark ordered, pointing toward the house. Woof sadly turned and started back, but as soon as Mark and Krissy weren't looking, he followed them again. This time they didn't see their dog behind them. Woof continued to trail his friends all the way to Mark's first-grade classroom.

No one noticed the dog peeking around the doorway as the students took their seats. Pretty soon the teacher spoke. "Good morning, class. My name is Mrs. Thomas," she said, standing at the chalkboard.

Suddenly Woof spotted Mark and barked a loud greeting to his master. All the children turned to see a scraggly mutt with a crooked ear, wagging his tail back and forth excitedly. A few of the children waved at him. Others burst out laughing as they pointed to the confused dog.

Mark was surprised and embarrassed. *Oh no!* he thought. *How did Woof get in here?*

Before he had a chance to react, a big kid in the back jumped out of his chair and lunged toward the dog. Woof became frightened and ran down the hallway.

"Catch that mutt!" someone shouted as the dog dashed by the office.

The principal and two teachers began chasing Woof through the building. The dog skidded around a corner and came to the end of the hall. Now he was trapped! The principal and teachers quickly surrounded Woof while one of them tied a rope around his neck. He was then led into the

office and put in a corner. Woof knew he had done something wrong. He also knew he should have listened to Mark and Krissy when they told him to go home. Now he was in trouble, and there was no way out!

Pretty soon a white van from the city pound stopped in front of the school. Two men got out and went into the office. Unfortunately, Woof's dog tag had come off. So the men led him outside and into the back of the van.

Woof didn't know why he was being taken away from the school. But he had a feeling the men were not taking him back to his home on Maple Street. And he was right.

Meanwhile, Mark and Krissy searched the school grounds looking for their lost dog. All during recess they looked for Woof, but he had simply disappeared. Finally they decided he had probably gone home.

If only the children had known Woof was in serious trouble!

The big van pulled in front of a small building. Then the
men took Woof to a room in the back and shoved him inside
a wire cage. The cage was dirty and uncomfortable, and the
room smelled awful! Six other dogs were around him in cages
like his. They barked and howled miserably. Woof had never
been to a pound before—even when he was a stray before the
Petersons adopted him. He hated this place and wanted more
than anything to go home.

Woof anxiously looked around the room at the scrawny
dogs in their cages. There was a golden retriever, a bulldog,

and a Chihuahua among the others. Right next to him lay an old, toothless hound. He was skinny and looked tired. Although several flies buzzed around his nose, he didn't even try to fight them off. Only his eyes moved as he lay on the floor of his uncomfortable cage.

Woof became more frightened as time went by. He wished he could have a good meal and be in his soft bed at home. And he wanted more than anything to see the Peterson family again. Would he ever find his way home? Would he ever run and play with Mark and Krissy again? Woof rested his head on his front paws.

After a long time an assistant came in with a large bucket. He went around to the cages and dumped some of the contents into each dish. Woof sniffed at the food, but he didn't want to eat it. For the first time in his life, Woof had lost his appetite. He could only think about how much he missed his family.

Back at the Peterson house, Mark and Krissy had come home and found that Woof was not there. By six o'clock they were very worried. Mr. and Mrs. Peterson tried to be hopeful, but deep inside they were worried too. Where could Woof be? He had never run away before.

By bedtime the children were in tears.

"Let's pray for Woof, shall we?" Mother suggested.

Mark and Krissy knelt down by their beds and asked the Lord to protect their pet. They also prayed that the Lord would help them to find Woof soon.

The Petersons felt better after they had given the problem to Jesus. It made it easier for them to sleep that night, but they still missed their special friend.

The next morning while the children were getting ready for school, the telephone rang. Mrs. Peterson answered it. In a few moments she happily called Mark and Krissy downstairs.

"That was a boy named Brian from the school," she said. "He saw Woof being taken to the pound yesterday."

"The pound!" Mark and Krissy shouted at the same time. They were so glad Woof had been found that they weren't as angry about the pound as they might have been.

Mrs. Peterson called the school and told the secretary the children would be late. On the way to pick up Woof, Mark and Krissy thanked Jesus for answering their prayers.

When they arrived at the pound, they followed the sound of barking dogs into a back room. "Woof!" Mark shouted, spotting him in one of the cages.

Woof pricked up his crooked ear and jumped to his feet. He began wagging his tail and barking. He was so glad to see the children that he could hardly stay in one place! In a few seconds Mother came in with an assistant, who unlocked the cage. As soon as Woof was released, he jumped all over the children and licked their faces. The children were just as happy to see him!

But no one seemed to notice the other dogs, who had been watching the Petersons and their pet. As the family prepared to leave, Woof turned and looked at the toothless hound. The old dog gazed back at him with tired, sad eyes. Then Woof looked down the row of cages at the other dogs. They had stopped barking and were watching him quietly. They wished they had happy families to love them, too.

Mark turned and saw that Woof was not following them.
"Woof!" he called. "What's the matter?"

Krissy said, "Woof feels sorry for the other dogs."

"It is a sad situation," said Mother. "I wish we could do
something."

On the way to school the next morning, the two children talked about the homeless dogs. They knew their parents would never allow them to adopt all six. Besides, they already had Woof, and no dog could ever take his place. Still, the Peterson children were determined to help Woof's friends if they could. They just needed to think of a plan.

At school they asked students and teachers if anyone could help, but no one seemed to have any good ideas.

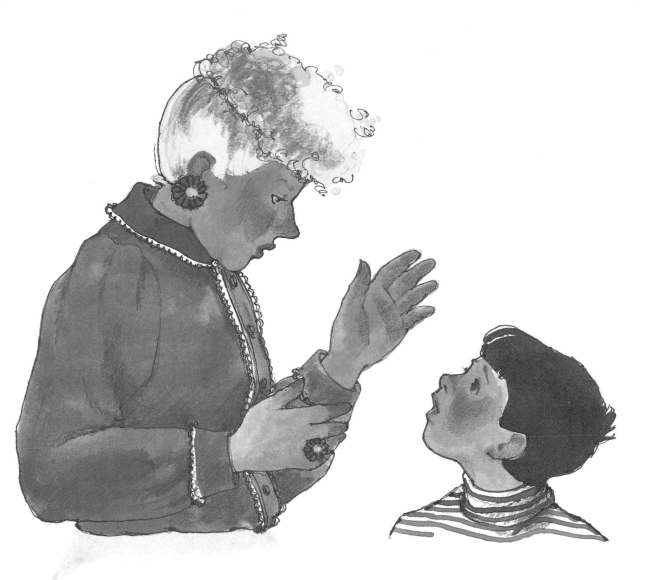

Finally Mark's teacher, Mrs. Thomas, came up with a suggestion. "Why don't you print some flyers and pass them around?" she asked. "That would be a great way to advertise, and it wouldn't cost very much."

"I like that idea!" Mark said. "Maybe we can find some families that will give those lost dogs a home."

When Mark told Krissy about Mrs. Thomas's idea, she agreed that it might work.

"Now we have to decide what we want the flyers to say," Mark said excitedly.

That afternoon the two children worked on the project at the kitchen table. When they were finished, this is what they had written:

PLEASE HELP save six homeless dogs at the city pound. These dogs are lonely and they need someone to love them. Here are the names we have given to the "Sad Six."

1. "Old Charlie": He's a little old, but very lovable hound dog.

2. "Freeway": a tiny Chihuahua that was picked up on the highway.

3. "Peppy": a gray terrier that runs and jumps all the time.

4. "Rusty": a golden retriever with a beautiful copper-colored fur coat.

5. "Trixie": a poodle who must have been in a circus act, because of all the tricks she can do.

6. "Rocky": a bulldog who could help protect your home.

PLEASE CALL Mark or Krissy Peterson if you could love and care for one of these dogs.

Phone: 782-4652   THANK YOU.

The next day Mrs. Thomas helped Mark make two hundred copies of the flyer in the school library. He put them on bulletin boards, lockers, and doorways. Between classes Mark and his friend Barney Martin handed them out to students as they went to the playground. Together they gave away most of the flyers by the end of the school day.

Mark finished distributing the rest of them around the neighborhood. Even Woof helped! He carried them in his mouth and dropped them on doorsteps.

That evening the Petersons' phone kept ringing off the hook! Mark and Krissy returned forty-two phone calls from students and teachers who had seen the ad.

"Imagine that," Mother sighed. "Forty-two calls for only six dogs."

Mark didn't respond as he looked down at the floor.

"What's the matter?" Father asked.

"The phone calls have been for only five dogs—not six. No one wants Old Charlie," Mark said sadly. "I just can't stand to leave him alone in that wire cage. He looks so pitiful."

"Don't feel guilty, Son," said Father. "You provided five homeless animals with a place to live. You should feel proud of yourself."

Mark nodded his head. "I guess you're right. Maybe someone will change his mind about Old Charlie."

"I wouldn't count on that," said Father. "An old dog wouldn't be of much use to anyone. And it might be hard to take care of him."

Deep inside, Mark knew his father was right. There was little chance anyone would want to adopt such an animal. All Mark could do was hope someone would call.

The next day was Saturday. Mark and Krissy got up early so they could pick up the dogs and deliver them. Mark's friend Barney Martin had called and said his father would drive his pickup truck to get the dogs. Everything had worked out perfectly—well, almost.

At nine-thirty Mr. Martin and Barney arrived at the Petersons' home. The children put Woof in the back of the truck, and they crawled into the front. It was a little crowded, but they managed to squeeze in. Pretty soon the truck pulled into the parking lot of the pound.

"Excuse me," Mark said, walking through the double doors at the entrance. "My name is Mark Peterson, and I've come to pick up five of the dogs."

The middle-aged woman at the desk looked a little surprised. "Right this way," she directed.

By this time Krissy and the Martins had caught up with Mark. Woof circled the room, sniffing the air. He remembered being there just a few days before. It was not a good memory.

Mr. Martin signed the papers and paid the small fee while the children and Woof walked down the hallway. The dogs had been barking and howling, but they stopped when they saw the children. How happy they were when the woman unlocked their cages! Five very excited dogs barked and ran around the room. The children laughed at the sight of them. But in a few moments their laughter stopped.

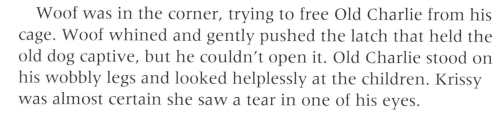

Woof was in the corner, trying to free Old Charlie from his cage. Woof whined and gently pushed the latch that held the old dog captive, but he couldn't open it. Old Charlie stood on his wobbly legs and looked helplessly at the children. Krissy was almost certain she saw a tear in one of his eyes.

"I can't stand to look," she said.

"Me either," Mark agreed. "Come on, let's go."

The three children and the rest of the dogs headed toward the truck. Woof took one last look at his tired, old friend and slowly left the room.

Five dogs barked happily in the back of the truck—but not Woof. He was still sad about the old hound dog. Woof understood what it was like to feel unwanted and unloved. Before he was adopted by the Peterson family, he had traveled the streets alone, with no one to love. He wished he could do something for the poor dog, but it was beyond his control.

One by one the children delivered the dogs to the families that wanted them. When the last of the "sad five" had a home, Mark and Krissy said good-bye to the Martins and thanked them for their help. The children felt happy as they walked home, but they hadn't forgotten about the sixth dog—worn-out, pitiful Old Charlie.

Just then Mark and Krissy noticed an elderly man walking toward them with the help of a cane. He staggered along the street and met them as they reached the driveway of their house. He was holding one of the flyers Mark had printed.

"Are you the Peterson children?" he asked.

"Yes," Mark answered.

The old man smiled. "My name is Mr. Robbins, and I live down the street. I want to ask you about the advertisement for the dogs."

"I'm sorry, mister, but all the dogs have been given away," Mark said. "There's only one left, and he's an old hound dog. I don't know if you'd be interested him."

"Why, that's just the kind of dog I *am* interested in," Mr. Robbins replied. "You see, I'm old too. I've lived a good life, but I just don't have very much energy anymore. I think an old hound and I would get along just fine. I could use a needy friend."

Mark and Krissy grabbed each other and shouted.

"That's great!" Krissy exclaimed. "Old Charlie is still at the pound. If you'd like, I'm sure my parents would give you a ride."

"Thank you," Mr. Robbins said. "I'm far too old to drive anymore. But if your mom and dad will give me a ride, I would like to take a look at the dog."

Mark and Krissy ran into the house to tell their parents the
good news. Their mother and father were delighted and
agreed to drive Mr. Robbins to the city pound that afternoon.

Later that day the Peterson family and Mr. Robbins pulled
into the parking lot. Even Woof went along for the ride.

They followed Mr. Robbins into the room where Old
Charlie lay. The Petersons and Woof stood at the door and

watched as the elderly man slowly made his way to the cage.
He gently reached inside to stroke Old Charlie on the head.
There seemed to be an instant bond of love between the man
and the dog as their eyes met for the first time. With his
warm, pink tongue, Old Charlie licked Mr. Robbins's hand.
After a few moments Mr. Robbins looked up. "Unlock the
cage," he said to the assistant. "I'll take him."

Mark and Krissy could hardly keep from shouting as Old
Charlie was released from his miserable cage. Even Woof
stood with his tail thumping against the wall.

Mr. Robbins turned toward the family and smiled. "This
old hound will make a perfect friend for me. Given our ages,
we'll probably get to heaven about the same time."

The Petersons followed behind as Mr. Robbins and Old Charlie limped out the door and down the hall together. Mark wiped away a tear. "Do you know what?" he asked. "I believe God even cares about an old dog like Charlie, don't you?"

"Yes," Krissy answered. "And if he cares that much about a dog nobody wanted, just think how much he must love you and me! He loved us so much that he sent his only Son to die for us. That's the most special love there is."

WOOF GOES TO SCHOOL

Theme: God loves everyone, so we should love each other.

Talking about Woof

Why was Woof taken to the city pound?

How did Woof show love toward Old Charlie?

Talking about Mark and Krissy

What did Mark and Krissy do to show love toward the dogs at the pound?

At the end of the story, Old Charlie was finally adopted and given a home. How did that remind the children of God's love for them?

Talking about Me

How did God show his love for you?

Plan ways that you can show love to family and friends today, including animal friends!

Reading What the Bible Says

For God so loved the world that he gave his one and only Son, that whoever believes in him shall not perish but have eternal life. *John 3:16*

Talking to God

Dear God, thank you for loving me enough to send your Son to die for my sins. Show me how to share your love with others.

    I want to pray for . . .

    Thank you for . . .

    I love you, God. In Jesus' name. Amen.

WOOF

AND THE
HAUNTED HOUSE

T H E M E

Think about the words you say.

Psalm 19:14

In the center of town, near Mark and Krissy Peterson's home, stood a spooky-looking house. Years ago it had belonged to a strange man whom people came to call Old Man Wilson. No one knew him very well, and he seemed to have no friends. Mr. Wilson had bent shoulders and long white hair. He walked around town very slowly with the help of a big black cane.

Mr. Wilson seemed even more strange as he grew older. He talked to himself when he walked along the sidewalk.

Sometimes he stood in his front yard for a long time, just looking into space. Of course, the children in that part of town began to tell scary stories about the mysterious old man.

As the years went by, Mr. Wilson began to be sick more often. One night before his eighty-sixth birthday, he went to bed, and the Lord quietly took him to heaven. He had lived a very long life.

The next week a city workman came and boarded up the windows and doors so children would not go inside the old house. It was not a safe place to play.

All of this happened years before Mark and Krissy Peterson were born. By the time they came along, there was a great mystery in the town about Mr. Wilson's old house. No one had lived there since he died. You would be surprised by the scary stories the schoolchildren told one another. Parents sometimes let their kids believe the stories so they would stay away from the dark old house.

Mark, who was six years old, had heard all the tales. He wasn't sure he believed them, but the old place did look pretty scary. He and Krissy walked past the Wilson house every afternoon on the way home from school. *Someday,* Mark thought, *I'll find out what it looks like inside!*

One Friday afternoon Mark decided this was the day. He told his ten-year-old sister about it after school. "I don't know, Mark," she said. "I'm afraid of that house. I've heard it's haunted and a lot of strange things have gone on there."

Their dog, Woof, who had been lying on his bed, sat up and cocked his head from side to side.

Mark laughed at his sister. "That's silly! You're just a big coward. Please go with me. Besides, Mom won't let me go that far unless you come along."

Krissy thought for a moment. "Well . . . all right."

While she went to get her jacket and a flashlight, Mark telephoned his best friend, Barney Martin, and asked him to join them. Barney agreed to go, so the two children and Woof began walking toward his house.

Barney met them at the door, and he looked a little uneasy. "I decided not to go to the Wilson house," he said timidly. "My brother has heard all sorts of stories about kids getting

trapped and never getting out. He said some people have seen Old Man Wilson walking around the grounds and—"

"Oh, Barney," Mark interrupted. "You're just being silly!"

Woof barked and wagged his tail as if to agree.

Barney looked at the ground and put his hands in the pockets of his trousers. "Well, all right then. I'll go with you," he said, looking back up at his friends. "But if anything goes wrong, don't say I didn't warn you."

With that, the three children and Woof headed toward the old house. Barney froze when he caught sight of the rooftop. "I don't want to go any farther," he said nervously.

Mark was beginning to lose patience. "Barney, would you stop being such a scaredy-cat and come on?"

Barney caught his breath and continued to walk, but he would rather have been anywhere than near the old house.

By the time they got to the front yard, even Woof seemed a little uneasy as he sniffed the air. The children stood at the iron gate and gazed at the run-down house. It was surrounded by weeds and bushes. The windows and doors were nailed shut with boards that had been sloppily placed over the openings. The setting sun outlined the building with an orange glow as the trees swayed back and forth around its aging panels. Woof began to growl, and the hair stood up along his neck.

"Let's see if we can find a way to get inside," said Mark.

Krissy held her brother's arm as they crept slowly around the outside of the house. Woof trotted ahead of them and disappeared around the corner. In a second they heard him barking.

"Look! Woof found an opening!" Mark said excitedly as he rounded the corner.

Sure enough, a board had come loose from the side of the
house. "Let's go!" Mark exclaimed.

Barney gulped and held his breath as the three children
and Woof pushed their way through the opening.

Inside, the house was dark, and the air smelled musty.
Mark turned on the flashlight and held it up high so they
could see. Many mysterious shapes surrounded them! The
children listened to the wild beating of their hearts as they
looked around the cold, dusty room. Ancient pieces of
furniture were covered with sheets, and a grandfather clock

was no longer ticking. On the floor was Mr. Wilson's black
cane, and a pair of tiny wire eyeglasses lay on the table.
Everything looked as though someone had left in a hurry.

The children tiptoed across the creaky floor.

Mark picked up a picture of a woman with white hair. He
whispered, "This must have been Mr. Wilson's wife."

The children had almost forgotten how frightened they were when Woof suddenly stiffened and growled. The hair on his back stood straight up! Krissy grabbed her brother's arm tightly and gasped. "I'm scared!" she said.

"Me too!" Mark admitted.

Barney was so frightened he couldn't speak. He just stood there with his teeth chattering and his knees knocking.

As the three children clung to each other, Woof began

making his way upstairs, growling and sniffing the air. When he reached the second floor, he disappeared around the corner. In a few seconds he began barking loudly.

"Let's go see what he found," Mark whispered.

"No way!" Krissy said, shivering. "We should get out of here right away!"

"Yeah!" Barney said with a tremble in his voice. "Let's go!"

"But we can't leave Woof," Mark told them.

"Yes, but what if somebody is up there?" Krissy said with both hands over her face.

"We *have* to get Woof," Mark said. "He may be in trouble."

"Try to call him, Mark. Maybe he'll come," Barney suggested.

Mark went to the foot of the staircase and took a deep breath. "Woof. Come here, boy."

But Woof didn't come. He just continued to bark louder from a room at the top of the stairs.

"It's no use," Mark said firmly. "We have to go up there and get our dog. Besides, I want to know why he's barking."

The three children joined hands and huddled close together. Carefully they made their way up the rickety stairs, which squeaked with every step. Mark, in the lead, held firmly to the flashlight.

Suddenly Krissy screamed!

One of the old boards had given way, trapping her foot inside the stair. "Help me!" she cried.

Mark grabbed her by the hand. "It's all right," he assured her. "We'll get you out."

After several tugs, Mark and Barney managed to loosen Krissy's foot. Tears were streaming down her face, but she had only scraped her ankle.

The children started up the stairs again, being careful about where they stepped. When they reached the top, Mark aimed the flashlight down the dark hallway. They could still hear Woof barking in one of the rooms.

"Here, boy," Mark called. He called again, but Woof just kept barking and growling.

Finally the children reached the room where the dog was. Their hearts pounded like big bass drums as they peered inside, ready to run for safety at any moment. Woof was barking angrily at the closet door.

Krissy grabbed her brother's arm again. "Something is in that closet!" she exclaimed. Barney was shaking so much he could barely keep his balance.

Suddenly a very loud crash came from inside the closet, and the door flew open! All three children screamed and jumped at the same time. They turned and ran toward the stairs.

"Get me out of here!" Barney shouted.

Woof came tearing past the children on the stairs and darted out the opening. The three kids scrambled for the exit too, all trying to get out at once. They didn't want to know who or what was chasing Woof!

They ran like the wind down Pine Street, with Barney leading the way. Their hearts were beating wildly, and sweat was dripping down their faces as they reached the driveway of the Peterson home. Woof had taken a shortcut and was already barking at the front door.

Mr. and Mrs. Peterson were startled as the three children and Woof came running into the house looking very frightened. Everyone began talking at once as the children tried to explain what happened.

"Wait a minute," Father interrupted. "One at a time, please."
Mark began by telling how the Wilson house was haunted.
Krissy and Barney told about the big crash that had come from
inside the closet. Even Woof was barking as loudly as he could.

After the children finished talking, Mr. Peterson called two neighbors to go with him to investigate the old house. While they were gone, Mother tried to comfort the children, who were still very upset. Woof seemed just as uneasy as he lay on his blanket, whimpering softly.

An hour later Mr. Peterson returned. The children jumped up and met him at the door. "What happened?" asked Mark.

Mr. Peterson smiled and said, "I think we solved the mystery of your haunted house. Let's sit down, and I'll tell you about it." The children sat on the edge of their seats and listened closely as Mark and Krissy's father talked.

"It looks as if a big yellow cat was snooping around the house and became trapped in the closet. Woof's barking must have frightened him so that he darted out of there and ran outside. We found him at the top of a nearby elm tree."

The children were greatly relieved. "I'm so glad the house isn't really haunted like everyone thinks," Krissy said.

"Me too," Barney added. "I thought we were all going to die in there."

Everyone laughed about being frightened by a cat.

"Now wait a minute," Father said. "I hope you kids learned a valuable lesson from this experience. Exploring that old house was not smart—someone could have gotten hurt. They knew how fortunate Krissy was that her accident on the staircase wasn't worse than it was. The children nodded in agreement.

"What we did was wrong, and we're sorry," Mark added. "But we're thankful that God protected us anyway."

The next morning Mr. Peterson took the children to a museum. They had fun looking at the old things on display. While they were there, they looked at pictures and read

books about Mr. Wilson. The children learned many things about him that were different from the bad stories they had heard. They found out that he was a good man who had given away a lot of money to help others.

"Weren't any of those awful stories true?" asked Krissy.

"No," Father replied. "Mr. Wilson was a fine Christian gentleman. He just lived longer than his family and friends. Because he was old and lonely, he seemed much different from the way he really was."

Later that day Father got out the Bible and read from the book of James.

"You see, children," he began, "gossip can be a dangerous thing. Many people have been hurt by stories about them that weren't true. In James chapter 3 we read: 'Those who control their tongues can also control themselves in every other way.'" Father continued, "'The tongue is a small thing, but what enormous damage it can do.'"

"Just like with Mr. Wilson," Krissy said. "Someone made up a scary story about him and his house, and soon the whole town believed it."

"That's right," Mr. Peterson said. "We should always be careful not to believe rumors, and we should not repeat them to others."

"I'm sure I would have liked Mr. Wilson," Mark said.

"Me too," Krissy agreed. "He wasn't at all like I heard."

"He might even have liked Woof," said Mark, stroking the fur on his dog's head.

Mr. Peterson smiled. "He probably would have," he said thoughtfully. "In fact, I'm *sure* he would have—doesn't everybody?"

WOOF AND THE HAUNTED HOUSE
Theme: Think about the words you say.

Talking about Woof

When Woof was barking at the closet, what was inside?

When the closet door flew open, was Woof afraid? Was there a good reason to be afraid?

Talking about Mark and Krissy

Why did Mark and Krissy think Mr. Wilson's house was haunted?

How did the stories about Mr. Wilson make the children feel about him?

How did their trip to the museum change the way they felt?

Talking about Me

What should you do if you hear a bad story about someone? Should you believe it? Should you repeat the story to others?

When you're tempted to gossip about someone, what does God want you to do instead?

Reading What the Bible Says

May the words of my mouth and the thoughts of my heart be pleasing to you, O Lord. *Psalm 19:14*

Talking to God

Dear God, help me to be careful about what I say in front of others. And help me to watch what I think about too. Let everything I say, think, and do be pleasing to you, God.

    I want to pray for . . .

    Thank you for . . .

    I love you, God. In Jesus' name. Amen.

WOOF

AND THE MIDNIGHT PROWLER

THEME

Don't judge only by what you see.

1 Samuel 16:7

"Wake up, Krissy!" Mark Peterson called to his sister across the hall. "We don't want to be late to Grandma's today."

Grandma Peterson had one of the best farms in Idaho. It was filled with interesting animals, fruit trees, and farm equipment. Mark and Krissy loved to ride the tractors and help with the chores. They always had fun at Grandma's farm.

After breakfast the family piled into the station wagon, and Father began backing the car down the driveway.

"Wait!" Mark cried, glancing around him. "Where's Woof?"

As if responding to the question, a shaggy mutt with a crooked leg sped across the front yard and bounded into the back of the car, knocking over two suitcases.

Krissy patted the dog on the head. "Sorry, Woof. We just couldn't forget to take *you!*" Woof licked her face.

On the way to the farm, Father suggested that the family read the Bible and pray. The Petersons often did that on long car trips. Their faith was very important to them.

So Mrs. Peterson read the story of how David was the youngest and smallest of his brothers. But God still wanted him to be king. "Our heavenly Father doesn't judge us by how we look or how things appear to be," said Mrs. Peterson. "What he cares about most is what's in our heart."

Father then led the family in prayer and asked God to be with them on their trip to the farm.

After devotions the children read books and played games, but it wasn't long before they got tired of sitting in the crowded car.

"I'm thirsty!" Mark complained.

"Me too, and I have to go to the bathroom," Krissy added.

"Now, children, be patient. I'm sure there will be a gas station up the road," Mrs. Peterson said.

Even Woof seemed uncomfortable as he sat panting in the backseat.

Before long, the Peterson car pulled into a service station. Father put gas in the tank while the children bought soda pop and played with Woof. They hardly noticed the pickup truck that pulled up beside them.

A large man got out of the truck and went inside the station. In the back of the truck were twin boys who looked like pure trouble. Their hair was uncombed, and their faces were grubby. They probably hadn't washed with soap and water for days. Mark and Krissy didn't pay much attention, although they wondered why the boys kept looking at them and whispering.

Then it happened. Just as Woof was running to catch a stick Mark had thrown, one of the boys hurled a rock from the back of the truck. It hit Woof in the shoulder with a thud. He let out a yelp and rolled end over end. Mark and Krissy gasped as they ran over to their injured dog to see how badly he was hurt. In the background they could hear the boys laughing wildly.

Krissy marched over to her father to tell him what had happened. But before she could explain, the man got back into his truck and drove away from the gas station.

"Oh, no!" Krissy cried.

"What happened?" Father asked, seeing the tears in his daughter's eyes.

After Krissy explained what the boys had done, Mr. Peterson became very upset. "I can't believe anyone would do something so cruel to an innocent animal." Then he walked over to Woof and checked for broken bones. After finding none, he cleaned the blood off the dog's fur and gave him some fresh water to drink.

Jake, the gas-station attendant, noticed how sad Woof looked. "That was a rotten thing to do," he said, patting the straggly head. "Them Harper boys is always causin' trouble around here. Someone needs to take a stick to their backsides."

In a short while Woof appeared to be feeling better. The family climbed into the car again and said good-bye to Jake. Three hours later they reached the dirt road that led to Grandma Peterson's farm.

"We're almost there, kids," Mother said. "Get your things together."

100

Up ahead they could see an older woman waving to them excitedly.

"There's Grandma!" Krissy shouted.

They forgot all about the long ride as they tumbled out of the car and ran to greet her. Even with a sore shoulder, Woof was close at their heels, while Mr. and Mrs. Peterson followed at a slower pace. (Some adults don't like to run very much, as we all know.)

"Oh! It's so good to see you," Grandma said warmly as she hugged the children.

"It's been a long time since we were here last," said Mark. "Hey! I don't think you've met our great dog, Woof!"

He bent over to give his pet a hug while Grandma scratched her head and wrinkled her brow. "He certainly isn't a pretty sight! Look at that crooked tail! And those floppy ears!"

"Well, remember, Mom," Father said. "He did save your grandson's life."

Grandma smiled at Mark as she remembered how Woof had kept him from being hit by a car not long ago.

"Well, I don't see how a dog that ugly can be worth a whole lot, but he's welcome anyway," she laughed. "Come on inside. I've got dinner waiting."

While the family visited with Grandma, Woof began to explore the area. Since he had never been to a farm, there were many strange animals he had never seen before.

Woof was fascinated by the cows, pigs, and chickens. The chickens were not so thrilled to see Woof, of course. They cackled wildly and scurried to stay out of his way. But Woof

continued to chase them around the coop, playfully nipping
at their feathers. After a while he got bored with the chickens
and went on to explore the other sights and smells.

In the meadow he could see fields of wheat blowing gently
in the breeze and a tiny stream running through the center of
the farm. Woof completely forgot about his sore shoulder as
he chased rabbits and ran through the thick grass. This was
the most fun he had experienced in a long time!

He barely noticed it was getting dark as he explored the barns and sniffed the unusual smells that were everywhere. In the distance he heard Mark call his name. Maybe he had some table scraps to offer! Woof began trotting back to the farmhouse, exhausted from his adventurous afternoon.

Mark met him at the door. "Woof! Where have you been all this time?" Woof licked his hand happily.

"Grandma says you will have to sleep on the porch, but I made you a soft bed and gave you some food." Woof's ears pricked up. He loved to eat more than anything in the world.

Just then Krissy unlatched the screen door. "Mark, do you think it's safe out here for Woof?"

"I think so," Mark replied. "Grandma said he'd be all right.'

With that, the children gave their dog a pat and hurried off to bed. Woof circled his blanket three times, as dogs have done for thousands of years. He then curled up in a little ball. But Woof couldn't sleep. Hours passed and yet he lay still, listening to the crickets and an occasional hoot from an owl. Finally, drowsiness began to overtake him, and he drifted off to sleep.

No sooner had Woof closed his eyes than he heard a
strange noise from the chicken coop. He jumped up and
cocked his ears from side to side, his heart thumping rapidly.
After a few moments another noise echoed in the night,
followed by frantic squawking from the chickens. Woof
hurried to the coop, his eyes straining to see in the darkness.
As he peered inside, a strange scent drifted into his nostrils.

106

Suddenly he saw something move! A mean doglike creature was stalking in the darkness. He had chicken feathers on his nose, and his ears stood straight up. Woof didn't know the animal in the shadows was a coyote, but he understood that it was his enemy. He also knew the chickens belonged to the farm and the killer didn't. The coyote wheeled toward Woof and growled angrily. He crouched low, preparing to fight.

Meanwhile, the Petersons had also heard the noise and came outside with a flashlight.

"Woof! Here, boy!" Mark called. The coyote dashed past Woof in the darkness and made his escape. Woof stayed where he was because Mark had called his name. The Petersons hurried to the coop and turned on the light. There stood Woof, surrounded by a million feathers! The frightened chickens had escaped and were perched around the top of the coop.

"I knew it!" Grandma wailed. "That no-good dog has gotten into my chickens!"

Mark ran over and stared at the mess. "Woof! Why did you do it?" he cried.

"I can't believe it," said Father. "He's never tried to hurt anything before. I am very disappointed. Let's tie him up for tonight and decide what to do in the morning."

Krissy and Mark looked at each other sadly. They knew Woof was in great trouble. Grandma Peterson tried to be nice, but she was very angry at the ugly dog.

"Poor Woof," Krissy sighed. "Everything has gone wrong for him today."

For the rest of the night and the next day, Woof was kept tied to a fence post by a short rope. He was very unhappy because he couldn't trot around the yard and explore. He had never been tied up before and didn't like the feeling. In fact, the rope got so tangled around a bush that he could hardly move.

Krissy left with her mother and grandmother to pick berries in the meadow. Woof wanted to go with them and barked twice as they walked down the path, but they just told him to hush.

Then Mark passed by on his way to the barn with two farmworkers. Woof barked again, but they didn't hear him.

All day long he watched the children as they rode tractors and ran and played. Oh, how he wanted to be with them!

Woof knew the family was upset with him over something—Grandma was especially angry. Every time she passed him, she shook her finger and called him a "naughty dog!" It was a long, miserable day for Woof.

By the time evening came, everyone was tired and hungry. Woof watched as the family passed by him on the way to the house. After dinner Mrs. Peterson went outside to take Woof a bone and bring him some fresh water. His sad eyes made her feel sorry for him.

"We're going home tomorrow, boy," she said softly.

Woof wagged his tail and looked up at her hopefully. Mrs. Peterson petted him and then made her way back to the house.

That night Woof waited patiently for the children to come outside and say good night as they had before. Darkness fell on the countryside, and the minutes turned into hours. But still no one came to see him. Finally he gave up and lay down on the cool grass by the fence.

It began to get very late, but again Woof could not sleep. He knew the strange creature might return, only this time Woof was tied with a rope. What could he do? He kept his eyes fixed on the chicken coop and listened closely. The later it got, the more nervous the dog became. Anxiously he paced back and forth by the fence, staring into the black night.

Sometime after midnight a dark shadow moved near the coop. The prowler had returned! Woof's body tensed, and he pulled against the rope that held him captive. The shadow slipped to the door of the coop. Woof couldn't stand it. He heaved violently against the rope and growled angrily. Suddenly the rope broke and set him free!

Chickens in the coop were squawking and frantically flapping their wings. Woof raced toward the coop with all the energy he had. This time he didn't pause when he reached the door. The surprised coyote had no time to prepare before Woof was on him. There in the night the two animals began a fight to the death. Growling, biting, and tumbling through the darkness, Woof gave everything he had to the struggle.

The chickens scattered in terror, and a horse in a nearby barn neighed. Every animal on the farm knew there was a battle under way. Fortunately, so did the Petersons. The entire family seemed to run from the farmhouse at the same time. Even Grandma came running down the porch with her robe flying in the night air.

115

As Woof and the coyote fought, they knocked over a stack of empty feed barrels that stood by the door. The coyote was trapped inside the coop! When he heard human voices, he stopped fighting and backed into a corner. Woof, breathing heavily, stood guard with his head low. The coyote had finally had enough. He had never tangled with a fighter like this dumb-looking dog. He wanted no more battle!

The Petersons reached the coop and directed a flashlight over the barrels. Spotting Woof and the coyote, Grandma gasped in shock. "Oh, my!" she said. "I'd better get a rope."

With that, she headed toward the barn. The rest of the family stayed outside and kept watch to make sure the coyote didn't get away. Mark and Krissy were relieved that Woof was not responsible for threatening the chickens the night before.

When Grandma returned with the rope, Father managed to toss it around the coyote's neck. After a struggle, Mr. Peterson tied the animal in the barn. It was a very exciting night for the whole Peterson family!

As they made their way back to the house, Mark suddenly realized that Woof wasn't with them.

"Where's Woof?" he asked.

They found their dog sitting on the front porch in the dark, licking his wounds. Mark hugged Woof affectionately and untied the length of rope that still hung around his neck. "You're the best dog anyone ever had!" he said happily.

Even Grandma was pleased with the heroic dog. "I'm sorry I scolded you for something you didn't do," she apologized, patting him on the head. "I'm going to give you some nice, juicy steak bones!"

Woof panted happily and wagged his tail. He wasn't certain what Grandma had offered him, but her voice sounded kind.

"I'm sure glad Woof wasn't the one that upset those chickens," Father said. "I was afraid we could never have turned him loose again, even at home."

The family brought Woof into the farmhouse to clean and disinfect his wounds. Then they fed him and gave him a warm bed—in the *house* this time. He was very happy to be loved by the family again.

"Well, let's get some sleep," Father said, yawning. "We've had enough excitement for one night."

The next morning Mr. Peterson called the Department of Fish and Game to ask if they would come pick up the coyote. They said they would be there at noon to take him far away. Then they would let him go.

The children and Woof played in the field until the men from the Department of Fish and Game arrived. Woof was the first one to greet them, making a dash toward their truck and barking happily. Everyone watched as the men led the coyote from the barn into the truck. When the coyote saw Woof, he growled angrily.

"It's all right, Woof," Mark said kindly. "There's no way he can cause any more trouble, thanks to you."

After the truck left, Father announced it was time to pack the car and leave for home.

When everything was taken care of, Grandma came outside to tell them good-bye. "Thanks for coming to visit, and please come again soon," she said, hugging the children. "And don't forget to bring Woof. He's the bravest and smartest dog I've ever seen. I'd love to have him around the farm all the time."

As if understanding her kind words, Woof licked her hand.

"That's our hero!" Mark added, giving Woof a hug.

After everyone had said good-bye four more times, Grandma stood watching as the car made its way down the dirt road toward the main highway. In the distance she could see a small animal poke his furry head out the rear window and look back at her. His strange ears wiggled in the breeze.

"That dumb-looking dog really is special," she said to herself. "I'll miss him."

On the way home Mrs. Peterson opened the Bible again for devotions.

Krissy suddenly thought of the story about God wanting David to be king. "Hey! Remember how we learned that God looks at us on the inside and not the outside? Well, we were all judging Woof when we thought he was after Grandma's chickens. He really wasn't, but we were looking at the outward appearance."

"That's true," said Father. "It's important not to judge people—
or dogs—too quickly. Things are not always as they seem."

Later that day the Petersons stopped at Jake's gas station
again. As they drove up to a pump, they couldn't believe their
eyes. The Harper twins were at the vending machine buying
soda pop!

Father opened the door and intended to talk to the boys,
but Woof had a better idea. He jumped out of the car and
headed for the twins. As the boys were putting coins into the
machine, Woof ran up behind them and let out his loudest,
deepest, meanest bark. The twins jumped two feet into the air
and screamed in terror. They turned and ran to their truck as
fast as they could, with Woof nipping at their feet.

Krissy and Mark looked at each other and burst out
laughing. Mr. and Mrs. Peterson had a hard time hiding their
smiles too. And would you believe—even Woof had a smile
on his doggy face!

WOOF AND THE MIDNIGHT PROWLER

Theme: Don't judge only by what you see.

Talking about Woof

Everyone thought Woof was trying to hurt Grandma's chickens. What was he really trying to do?

Did he get punished in an unfair way? How?

Talking about Mark and Krissy

Did Mark and Krissy wonder if Woof was guilty? How do you know?

What did the children learn about judging too quickly?

Talking about Me

Have you ever judged someone in an unfair way?–

Aren't you glad that God never does that to anyone?

Reading What the Bible Says

Man looks at the outward appearance, but the Lord looks at the heart.
1 Samuel 16:7

Talking to God

Dear God, teach me to be kind and understanding as I look at other people. I want to be more like you.

> I want to pray for . . .
> Thank you for . . .
> I love you, God. In Jesus' name. Amen.

WOOF

AND THE
NEW NEIGHBORS

THEME

Love your enemies.

Matthew 5:44-45

It was a warm Saturday morning as the Peterson family sat down to breakfast.

"Guess what?" said six-year-old Mark, reaching for a muffin. "Barney said some people bought the house next door, and they're moving in today."

Father smiled as he turned a page of the newspaper. "That's good," he said warmly. "That house has been empty for six months. It will be nice to have some new neighbors."

The conversation was interrupted by a shaggy-haired mutt with a crooked leg and one floppy ear. He bounded into the room with a red ball in his mouth and placed it by the children's feet, as if wanting to play.

"Not now, Woof," ten-year-old Krissy laughed.

Woof stayed near the table, hoping a bite of food would drop onto the floor.

"I hope the new family next door will have kids our age," said Mark.

"Why don't you both be there to greet them when they arrive," suggested Mother. "I'm sure they'd like that."

The children agreed and went outside to play catch with Woof.

An hour later a huge yellow moving van stopped in front of the house next door. Mark and Krissy quit playing ball and watched as the tires screeched to a stop at the curb. Behind the van was an old pickup truck carrying three passengers. They pulled into the driveway.

"Boy! That truck looks familiar," said Krissy, straining her eyes to get a closer look.

The moving van backed into the driveway and hid the truck from view.

"Come on!" said Mark, grabbing his sister by the sleeve.

The two children moved closer to the van and stood by an

old oak tree in their yard. Even Woof seemed curious as he followed at their heels.

The children could hear voices, and doors being opened and shut. Soon a husky man walked in front of the van, carrying two boxes to the front door.

Suddenly Woof growled and began to bark loudly.

"What is it, boy?" Mark asked.

The hair on the dog's back stood up as he looked straight ahead. Two young boys walked past the van and up the driveway. Mark and Krissy looked at each other and gasped out loud. *"The Harper twins!"* they shouted at the same time.

Woof continued to bark. He remembered those boys very well. They had hit him in the shoulder with a rock at a gas station last summer. He had been sore for four days, and he was still angry about it.

"I can't believe it!" Mark exclaimed. "Those awful Harper twins are moving in *next door!*"

"Come on. Let's go tell Mom and Dad," Krissy said.

The two children ran through the front door and into the living room, with Woof close behind.

"What's the matter?" asked Father, putting on his glasses.

Mark caught his breath and said, "Remember last year when two mean boys threw a rock at Woof while we were at a gas station?"

Mr. and Mrs. Peterson nodded.

"Those boys are our *new neighbors!*" Krissy wailed.

The two parents frowned in disbelief.

"Are you sure?" Mother asked.

"Yes!" Mark and Krissy said at the same time.

"Come look out the window, and you'll see!" said Krissy.

Woof continued to growl as the Petersons drew back the curtain and peered through the glass. Next door they could see two scruffy-looking boys in matching overalls unloading boxes from the van.

"They *are* the Harper twins!" Father said.

"What are we going do?" Mark asked.

"You should do what any neighborly person *would* do," Mother suggested. "Go over and say hello." Mrs. Peterson noticed the unhappy look on their faces. "Go on," she repeated. "Wouldn't you want to be welcomed if you moved into a new neighborhood?"

The two children looked at each other. "I suppose," Krissy said. "Come on, Mark, let's go."

The children and Woof went back outside and over to the big yellow van. Woof was still stiff legged and tense.

In a few moments the twins came out of the house to get another load. When they saw Mark and Krissy, they stopped and looked very surprised.

Krissy cleared her throat. "Hello," she said in a friendly voice. "I suppose you remember us from the gas station a while back."

The boys did not answer as they continued with their work.

"I'm Mark Peterson, and this is Krissy," said Mark. "And I'm sure you remember Woof," he chuckled.

133

The two boys still did not answer. Finally one of them said, "This here's Billy, and I'm Bobby. And over there by the fence is old Butch."

The Peterson children looked at the large bulldog that was tied to the gate.

"You best keep your mutt away from old Butch," Bobby sneered. "He just might make a meal out of him." The two boys burst out laughing.

Woof growled angrily at the twins. He would never hurt them, but he knew these boys were troublemakers.

The twins continued to laugh as Mark and Krissy turned and headed back to the house. They were very upset at how the boys had treated them, but they were even *more* upset that Billy and Bobby Harper were here to stay!

That night as the Peterson children were getting ready for bed, Father came upstairs to say good night.

"Why did the Harper twins have to move in next door?" Krissy complained.

"Wait and give them a chance," said Father. "But for now, I'd stay away from them. Maybe you can make friends with them later. And, Mark, keep Woof away from their dog! He looks pretty mean."

Much later that night, the entire Peterson family was awakened by a strange sound outside. It was a loud clanking noise.

Woof was downstairs in seconds, clawing at the door to get out. He wanted to protect his territory.

"What *is* that?" Krissy asked nervously.

"I don't know," Mark replied.

Again and again the sound came from the front yard, and it seemed to be moving. Mr. and Mrs. Peterson met the children at the foot of the stairs.

"Everyone stay inside," Father instructed. "Woof and I will check to see what's going on."

"Be careful," Mrs. Peterson warned.

In a couple of minutes Father returned to the house.

"What is it?" Mark and Krissy asked impatiently.

"Someone tied a can to a cat's tail," Father said with disgust. "The poor thing is scared to death. I need to get some scissors to cut the string."

Mark and Krissy went outside with him as he cut the can off the frightened cat. The poor kitty climbed the nearest tree after it was released.

"I bet I know who did this," said Krissy angrily. "It was Billy and Bobby Harper!"

"Possibly," agreed her father. "But you don't know for sure. Let's all go back to bed and get some rest."

The Peterson family was soon fast asleep again, but Woof still felt tense. He lay awake the entire night at the foot of Mark's bed, waiting for more trouble. But the rest of the night was peaceful.

When morning came, everyone got dressed for church.

Woof watched as the family climbed into the car and drove away. He was still on the porch when something caught his eye! Billy and Bobby Harper were creeping along the side of their house. Each of them was holding something in his hand. Woof didn't know these objects were slingshots, but he knew the boys were up to no good. Woof followed them at close range as they ran and hid behind a bush in a neighbor's yard.

One of the twins stood up and placed a rock in his slingshot. Then he pulled it back and aimed. In a flash the rock flew through the air and crashed through one of Mrs. Perry's windows. The impact sent glass shattering in all directions, and all the way down the street you could hear Mrs. Perry scream. By the time she got to the front door, the boys had made their escape.

Some neighbors heard the noise and came out to their front yards, but no one had seen who broke the window. No one, that is, except Woof! But there was nothing he could do.

When the Peterson family returned, they heard about Mrs. Perry's broken window. Mark and Krissy suspected the Harper twins, but their father pointed out that it could have been an accident.

Woof was becoming very upset. He was angry about all the trouble the boys were causing around the neighborhood, but he didn't know what to do. He paced back and forth around the backyard. Finally he stopped to get a drink from his water dish. No sooner had he begun lapping the liquid than he spit it out again—hacking and coughing.

When Mark walked outside, he saw Woof coughing and picked up the dish to see what was wrong.

"This smells like vinegar!" he exclaimed. "Those nasty twins must have ruined Woof's water with vinegar!"

When Mark told his parents what the boys had done, they were also upset.

"This definitely wasn't an accident," Mr. Peterson said. "I think it's time I had a talk with the boys' father."

Mr. Peterson walked over to the Harpers' house and rang the doorbell. The husky man came to the door.

After introducing himself and shaking hands, Mr. Peterson explained about the mischief that had been going on in the neighborhood. But before he could finish the story, Mr. Harper interrupted him angrily.

"Are you sayin' you think my boys is responsible fer all this?" he asked.

"Well . . . I . . ." Mr. Peterson was taken by surprise.

"My boys is good kids. Ain't no way they'd be doin' them

awful things. Mister, I reckon you got the wrong house."
With that, he shut the door.

As Mr. Peterson was walking away, he could see Billy and
Bobby Harper snickering by the window. *Those naughty boys,*
he murmured to himself.

Mark was putting some fresh water in Woof's dish when
his father returned.

"What happened, Dad?" he asked.

Mr. Peterson shook his head. "Their father didn't believe
me," he said. "We will just have to be more watchful."

For the next few days there were constant complaints around the neighborhood. Mark's friend Barney found a flat tire on his bicycle when he was leaving for school. Then Mrs. McCurry noticed her daisies had been trampled. Mr. Gosset discovered his big tree was covered in wet toilet paper. And a For Sale sign had been moved from a nearby house. The neighbors around Maple Street were in an uproar! But who was to blame? No one had seen the culprits.

One afternoon when the Peterson family had left with some friends, Woof stretched out behind the house in the sun. He could hardly wait for the children to return so he could go for a walk or play a game of catch.

Suddenly Woof's ears pricked up. A hissing sound had come from the garage! Woof trotted over to the side door and peered around the corner. There, crouched low by the Petersons' car, were Billy and Bobby Harper. They had let the air out of three tires! The two boys didn't see Woof as they crept over to the last tire to finish the job.

Woof knew he had to think fast! This would be a perfect opportunity to catch the boys, but how could he keep them in the garage until the Petersons returned? Anxiously Woof looked around the doorway. There, above him, was a tiny latch that hung just within his reach.

Quickly Woof nudged the door shut and pushed the latch down with his paw. The Harper twins were trapped inside!

"Let us out of here!" the boys yelled, banging on the door with their fists. Woof stood guard by the door, pacing back and forth and barking for help. But the Petersons had not returned home yet.

147

Suddenly Woof sensed he was in great danger. He wheeled around to see Butch coming after him! Butch bolted toward Woof with all his might.

Woof backed up against the garage door and braced himself for the attack. But just before the angry bulldog could pounce on him, a voice called from across the yard.

"Butch! Come here!" Mr. Harper commanded.

The bulldog skidded to a stop when he heard his name called.

"I said to come here *now!*" Mr. Harper repeated. Old Butch had obviously given up the fight, for he turned and headed back toward his master. "I thought I saw you leave the yard a minute ago," Mr. Harper said, grabbing his pet by the collar. "What are you doing here?"

Woof was greatly relieved that Butch had been called off. That could have been a terrible fight.

Just then the Peterson family returned in their friends' car.

"What's going on?" Mr. Peterson asked as he walked up the driveway.

Before he could get an answer, a loud noise came from the garage.

"What was *that?*" asked Krissy.

"It sounds like someone banging on the garage door," said Mother.

As the Petersons and Mr. Harper hurried toward the garage, they could hear voices inside.

"Let us out of here!" the boys yelled, continuing to bang on the door.

Woof stood guard as Mr. Peterson unlatched the lock that held them captive. As soon as they were free, Billy and Bobby Harper pushed their way out the door and into the yard. Their faces were hot and sweaty from being locked in the stuffy garage, and their hands were black from tampering with the tires.

Krissy gasped as she peered through the garage door.

"Why, they let the air out of our tires!" she exclaimed.

The boys lowered their heads in shame as everyone surveyed the damage.

"Did you boys do this?" asked Mr. Harper.

"Yeah, Pa, we done it," answered Bobby, who still hadn't looked up.

"Don't you think you owe these people an apology?" his father asked.

"We're sorry," said the twins at the same time.

"Now get on home, you two!" ordered Mr. Harper.

The boys took off running toward their house.

"I'm awful sorry about what my boys done to yer car," said Mr. Harper. "I'm also sorry for not believin' you when you was sayin' my boys was causin' trouble. But I'll talk with them about this and make sure they don't bother you no more."

"I'd appreciate that," said Mr. Peterson, extending his hand toward his neighbor. "And I hope we can be friends."

Mr. Harper smiled as he shook hands with his neighbor.

"Well, come on, Butch. Let's go," he said, motioning toward the gate.

The Petersons watched as Mr. Harper and his dog disappeared around the corner.

"I think Woof was the one who trapped the Harper twins in the garage!" exclaimed Mark, patting his dog on the head.

"Woof sure is a *good* dog," said Krissy.

"Why did you let Billy and Bobby Harper off so easily?" asked Mark, looking up at his father. "You didn't even get mad at them."

Father explained his reasoning. "Well, first of all, it is their father's place to discipline them. But there's another lesson to be learned from this. We'll talk about it after dinner tonight."

That evening, before bedtime, Mr. Peterson and the
children read these words spoken by Jesus about two
thousand years ago: "You have heard that it was said, 'Love
your neighbor and hate your enemy.' But I tell you: Love
your enemies and pray for those who persecute you, that you
may be sons of your Father in heaven."

"That means Jesus wants us to love everyone," said Mr.
Peterson. "He even wants his children to be friendly with
people who are not very nice. God loves the Harper twins as
much as he does us, even though he doesn't like the things
they do."

"How could God love *those* boys?" asked Mark.

"He made them, and he cares about them," said Father. "And there's another thought to consider—have you ever seen a mother at the Harper home?"

"No," said Krissy. "What do you think happened to her?"

"I don't know," said Father. "But they are having to grow up without a mother to love and care for them. We can only guess why they act the way they do. I believe they've had a pretty rough childhood. Whatever the cause, God knows about it and wants us to try to tell them about Jesus. Maybe we'll get that chance someday."

"I get it!" said Mark. "We'll never be able to tell them about Jesus if we stay mad at them all the time."

"That's right," said Mr. Peterson.

Mark and Krissy had a better attitude toward their new neighbors after talking with their father.

Woof didn't understand all those words, but he sure liked being in the Peterson family.

WOOF AND THE NEW NEIGHBORS
Theme: Love your enemies.

Talking about Woof

Why was Woof angry at the Harper twins?

How did he help to teach them a lesson?

Talking about Mark and Krissy

How did Mark and Krissy feel about having the Harper twins for neighbors?

What did Mr. Peterson say to change his children's attitudes toward the twins?

Talking about Me

Do you know someone who isn't very nice?

How does God want you to act toward people you don't like?

Reading What the Bible Says

Love your enemies and pray for those who persecute you, that you may be sons of your Father in heaven. *Matthew 5:44-45*

Talking to God

Dear God, I'm glad that you care about everyone. Help me to be like you by showing love to people who aren't easy to love.

    I want to pray for . . .

    Thank you for . . .

    I love you, God. In Jesus' name. Amen.

WOOF'S

BAD DAY

THEME

Always be ready
to talk about Jesus.

1 Peter 3:15

A warm breeze blew through the open windows of the Petersons' station wagon as it headed down the highway.

"Are we almost there, Dad?" asked the boy in the backseat.

"Not quite, Mark," answered his father, turning down the radio. "But there should be a road sign coming up soon."

After a few miles the Petersons saw an old wooden sign that read "Big Pine Recreational Campground."

"Just a half mile to go!" exclaimed ten-year-old Krissy, closing the book she'd been reading.

The two children kept close watch as their car turned off the highway and headed up the mountain trail. They had looked forward to this trip for a long time, and now the fun was about to begin!

A sleepy dog in the back lifted his head to look around. His crooked ear flopped over one eye as he took in the view, stopping for a few seconds to yawn.

"Wake up, Woof," said Mark, seeing his furry friend was not his usual perky self. "This is no time to sleep. We have a big day ahead of us."

Woof lay back down on the seat and sniffed at the picnic basket beside him. The smell of salami sandwiches held his attention for the time being. Woof was a very good dog, but he was greedy when it came to food. He loved to eat—almost anything!

Pretty soon the Petersons' station wagon pulled into the entrance.

"We're here!" shouted six-year-old Mark, opening the car door excitedly.

"Don't go too far," cautioned Mother as the two children dashed down the dirt road with Woof behind them.

Mark and Krissy stopped and looked at the beautiful scenery. Tall pine trees surrounded the campground, and the morning sun shone brightly on a nearby lake. Some campers were fishing, while others sat near their tents.

As Mark and Krissy went back to help set up camp, Woof trotted into the forest to explore. The fresh scent of pine needles and other strange smells tempted him to wander farther and farther away. But he wasn't worried. He would follow his own scent back to the campground.

While Woof wandered among the trees, something caught his eye. A tiny head about the size of a golf ball poked out of a dead log. Woof didn't know the creature was a chipmunk, but he found it fascinating! He walked closer to get a better look. The little animal stared out of the log with his nose wiggling rapidly.

Suddenly the chipmunk ducked back into the log. Woof peered into the opening, wondering why his little friend had disappeared so fast. He soon learned the reason why.

Grrroooowwlll! A mighty roar shook the forest. Woof wheeled around to see a large bear towering over him. The bear stood on his hind legs, saliva dripping from his fangs.

Woof's heart jumped into his throat! He ran back toward the camp as fast as he could go. The angry bear was right behind him. Fortunately Woof could run very fast, even with a crooked leg. He dodged around trees and through the thicket until finally he threw the bear off his trail.

162

The Peterson family was surprised when Woof came tearing
back into the campground. He dived for the tent and huddled
in the corner.

"What happened to *you?*" asked Krissy as she opened the
flap that served as a door.

"Woof looks like he's seen a ghost," laughed Mark, peering
inside. "Come on, boy. Let's go have some *real* fun!"

Woof crawled out of the tent and slowly followed Mark
and Mr. Peterson down to the lake. He was still frightened,
but he felt safer now that he was with the family.

While Mark and his father fished, Krissy and Mother went for a walk around the campground. They met some other families that were camping. Then they took out the lunch they had packed in the picnic basket.

It wasn't long before they figured out that a sandwich was missing. "Why, that sneaky little dog!" exclaimed Mother. "Doesn't he ever get enough to eat?"

"Never!" laughed Krissy. "But one of these days his appetite is going to get him into trouble."

Back at the lake Mark and his dad had caught five fish.
Woof was having a wonderful time splashing in the water. He
was also trying to catch a fish, but Mark made him stay far
away so he wouldn't scare off the trout.

Woof forgot about the bear as he jumped in and out of the
water. He was having so much fun that he almost didn't
notice the strange-looking animal watching him from behind
a bush. Woof walked to the shore and shook the water off his
fur. He spotted the odd-looking creature again and ran to
make a new friend.

It was the ugliest animal he had ever seen—a round ball with points all over its fur. Woof sniffed at him curiously. He had never seen a porcupine before. The porcupine didn't like Woof's company and tried to wobble away from the annoying dog. But Woof continued to run around him, barking playfully and nipping at his tail.

Mark heard his dog barking and came out of the water to check on him. Seeing the porcupine, Mark dropped his fishing pole and yelled, "Get back, Woof!" But it was too late. Poor Woof had sharp quills in his face, nose, and ears! He

yelped in misery as Mark and Father carried him back to the campsite.

Woof was really having a bad day!

"What happened?" asked Krissy.

"Woof had a little disagreement with a porcupine," answered Mr. Peterson. "We have to get these spines out quickly!"

Mother wasted no time in taking out her first-aid kit and going to work. She gently pulled out every quill and put medicine on the wounds. When she was finished, Woof felt a lot better. He was still a bit sore, though.

After lunch, Mark and Krissy asked their father if they could go on a hike.

"Yes, if you don't mind having me go with you," he replied. "There are bears around the campground."

"Stay here, Woof," instructed Mark as he patted his dog on the head.

"And don't get into any more trouble!" added Krissy.

Woof watched as the three headed off on their adventure. Ordinarily he would have wanted to go with them, but he had experienced enough excitement for one day. Besides, he thought that bear might be waiting for him out there somewhere.

As Woof lay on his blanket near the tent, a wonderful scent drifted into his nostrils. *Food!* he thought.

Quickly he glanced over to see what Mrs. Peterson was doing. She was in a lawn chair reading a book. Should he find out where the great smell was coming from? Why not? He followed the scent over a little hill and down to a row of picnic tables. People sitting at the tables had just enjoyed a good old-fashioned barbecue. The ribs smelled so good that it made Woof's mouth water. More than anything else, he wanted to bite into that great-smelling meat.

As Woof was trying to figure out how he could get some of the scraps, the people decided to leave. They threw all the plates into a huge trash can nearby. Woof couldn't believe his eyes! He waited patiently for the campers to pack their things, his mouth watering as he stood in the shadows. He was going to have the greatest meal of his life!

Finally he had the garbage to himself. He turned the can over, spilling the contents onto the ground. It was too good to be true! Woof began gobbling the scraps and chewing the bones as if he were starving.

He ate and ate—long after he was full. It was wonderful. Dogs don't usually smile, but Woof actually seemed to be grinning while he feasted. But after a while he started to feel miserable. His stomach began to hurt, and he became a little dizzy. He finally collapsed by the empty trash can, unable to move.

When the children returned from the hike, they looked around for their dog.

"Where's Woof?" asked Krissy nervously.

Mrs. Peterson glanced up from her book. "I'm not sure," she said. "He was with me a few minutes ago."

Just then a middle-aged man in a plaid shirt walked over to their camp. "Do you own a dog?" he asked.

"Yes, and he's missing," answered Father. "Have you seen him?"

"I believe so, and I think he's sick. He's lying on the ground as if he can't move."

"Let's go," said Mr. Peterson.

172

Krissy, Mark, and their parents followed the man to the picnic area.

"Oh my!" said Mother as she put her hands over her mouth.

Woof had indeed gotten himself into a mess this time. He lay flat on his back, his round belly twice its normal size. His four legs stood straight up in the air stiffly. Although Woof couldn't move, he rolled his big brown eyes toward his family when they walked toward him. Just a few splinters of dry bones lay on the ground near his head. Nothing else remained from his feast.

Mark and Krissy tried not to laugh as they lifted their dog and carried him back to the tent.

"You've really done it this time, Woof," said Mark as he struggled to carry the overfed animal. "I hope you've learned your lesson."

"You are a glutton, Woof!" Krissy added. "You should be ashamed of yourself for eating so much!"

Woof did feel very foolish. But whenever he thought of all those ribs with the fat and meat, he smiled again.

For the rest of the afternoon, Woof stayed on his blanket near the tent. Mark and Krissy spent their time playing Frisbee and horseshoes, but it wasn't as much fun without Woof.

As soon as the sun began to go down, Father started building a small fire.

"I'm starved!" said Mark. "Will dinner be ready soon?"

"Yes," answered Mother. "We're going to fry the fish you and Dad caught this afternoon."

"I don't think Woof will find the food very tempting," joked Krissy.

Woof looked over and wagged his tail a little bit. He was feeling better, but he still felt as if he weighed three hundred pounds.

All was peaceful around the campground as the Petersons thanked God for the food. They talked about their day as they enjoyed their meal by the fire. In the distance there were flickers of light where other campers had built small fires too.

Just as Mark was reaching for the marshmallows, a young boy walked up to their camp. "Hello," he said. "I'm Jason Foster. My dad was the one who told you about your dog."

"Oh yes," replied Mother. "We were just getting ready to roast marshmallows. Why don't you join us?"

"Thanks," Jason said as he took a seat next to Mark. "I came by to see how your dog is feeling. He seemed to be in bad shape this afternoon."

"Woof *was* in bad shape all right," agreed Krissy. "But he seems to be doing better now. Let's just say he's overloaded for the time being."

The Petersons laughed as they looked at their homely, overstuffed dog. Woof opened one eye and lifted his crooked ear, but he was too full to respond. Even the yummy smell of marshmallows didn't tempt him to move. Ordinarily Woof would have been begging for a few bites. But this time the thought of food didn't interest him.

For the rest of the evening the Peterson children talked by the fire with their new friend. They were having so much fun that they didn't notice it was nine o'clock.

"Mark, Krissy, it's time for bed," reminded Mother.

"I'd best be going anyway," Jason said, as he stood up and dusted off his jeans. "My dad is waiting for me."

"Wait a minute," said Krissy. "Since tomorrow's Sunday, we're going to have a church service in the morning. Would you like to come?"

"I don't know," replied Jason. "I've never been to church."

"It won't be a real church service," said Krissy. "We're just going to read the Bible and talk about God here on the mountain. How about it?"

"Well, I'll have to ask my dad," Jason answered.

"Be here at ten o'clock in the morning if you can come," said Mr. Peterson.

"Maybe," replied Jason. With that, he headed into the night.

Mark and Krissy snuggled into their sleeping bags and zipped them up all the way.

"I've had so much fun today!" exclaimed Krissy as she fluffed up her pillow.

"Me too," agreed Mark. "Even with all of Woof's mischief!"

"Shhhh," whispered Mother from the other side of the tent. "It's time to go to sleep."

The campfire smoldered and turned to ashes as the Petersons fell asleep under the stars.

When morning came, the family awoke to birds singing in the trees. Woof was already up and looking forward to breakfast. Mark found him by the lake, trying to catch a fish. His stomach was still oversized, but his energy had returned.

"Woof! Here, boy," called Mark. Woof was soaking wet as he bounded across the shore in the direction of his friend.

When they got back to the camp, Mother was frying eggs and sausage in a skillet over the fire. Woof licked his chops as he smelled the appetizing food.

"No, no," scolded Krissy. "You stay away from our breakfast." Woof looked disappointed as he sat down on his blanket.

When the Petersons finished eating, they looked up to see Jason and his dad coming toward them.

Mr. Peterson stood up and shook hands with Jason's father. "I'm glad you could join us," he said warmly.

"I'm not into religion very much," Mr. Foster commented. "But you're nice folks, and Jason told me how much fun he had here last night."

Everyone sat in a circle as Father opened the Bible and began to read from the Gospel of John. "For God so loved the world that he gave his one and only Son, that whoever believes in him shall not perish but have eternal life."

"What does that mean?" asked Mr. Foster.

Father explained how Jesus came to take away people's sin by dying on the cross. He said that Jesus loves each of us as if we were the only person on earth.

Jason and Mr. Foster asked lots of questions, and Mr. Peterson answered them by reading from the Bible. They closed their devotions with prayer, thanking God for all the things he had done for them.

Krissy turned to Jason and smiled. "I want you to have this," she said as she handed him her Bible.

"Thank you," Jason said gratefully. "I've never read the Bible before, but I will now."

"I have one last, special verse just for Woof," Mr. Peterson laughed. Bending down and looking straight into Woof's big brown eyes, Father quoted from Haggai 1:6, "You eat, but never have enough."

Woof didn't know why everyone was laughing at him. All he knew was that it was time to eat and he was hungry. But he wasn't interested in the doggie crunchies that lay in his bowl. He had his mind on something better!

While the Peterson family said good-bye to the Fosters, Woof trotted down to the lake. He was *determined* to catch a fish before it was time to go home. He splashed around in the water, looking beneath the surface for any kind of movement.

In a few moments Woof became very excited. A small dark shadow passed beneath him in the water. But before he could catch it, the creature rose to the surface. It was not a fish but a snapping turtle! It quickly lunged for Woof's tail, which was wagging just above the water. The turtle clamped down tightly with its powerful jaws.

Woof howled in pain! He twisted and turned in the water, but the turtle hung on. Woof ran up the road as fast as he could go—with the turtle bouncing along behind.

"Oh no, Dad!" said Mark. "Woof is in trouble again!"

Mr. Peterson hurried over to the dog and pried the turtle's jaws off his tail.

"We better put Woof in the car before he gets himself killed," laughed Krissy.

Soon the station wagon rattled down the dusty mountain trail.

"Well, at least one good thing came from Woof's overeating," Mother commented.

"What's that?" asked Mark.

"We never would have met Jason and his dad if it hadn't been for Woof's mischief. Because of it, we had a chance to tell them about Jesus."

"That's true," agreed Krissy, patting her dog on the head.

As the Peterson family laughed and talked about the trip, Woof poked his head out the rear window. The breeze felt good against his face. He thought about all the things that had happened that weekend and the lessons he had learned. They were lessons he would never forget. Soon a familiar scent interrupted his thoughts. Woof sniffed the air and became excited, leaning farther out the window.

Just then the Petersons' car drove past a sign that read "Arnold's Rib Joint—1/2 mile ahead." Woof's tail was wagging happily.

WOOF'S BAD DAY
Theme: Always be ready to talk about Jesus.

Talking about Woof

What are some of the reasons why Woof had a bad day?

Do you think he learned from his mistakes?

Talking about Mark and Krissy

Mark and Krissy were nice to Jason. How did that help Jason want to learn about God?

What are two ways that Krissy shared her faith with Jason?

Talking about Me

Name some people you know who don't know very much about Jesus.

Think about some ways you can help them learn about him.

Reading What the Bible Says

If you are asked about your Christian hope, always be ready to explain it.
I Peter 3:15

Talking to God

Dear God, I want to help my friends learn about you and your Son, Jesus. Show me what I can say that will help them understand how much you love them.

    I want to pray for . . .

    Thank you for . . .

    I love you, God. In Jesus' name. Amen.

WOOF
AND THE
BIG FIRE

THEME

Love unselfishly.

John 15:13

The hot sun beat down on the sidewalk as the Peterson children and their dog rounded the street corner. "Come on, Woof!" laughed Mark, pulling at the leash. "How many times do you have to stop?"

Woof paid no attention as he sniffed a fire hydrant.

"Maybe we should go back home," suggested Krissy. "It's too hot."

"You're right," agreed Mark. "Let's get some lemonade."

Just then the children saw their friend Fire Chief Jackson on the other side of the street. He had two beautiful Dalmatian dogs with him.

"Hello," he said as he came toward the children. "It's a little warm for a walk, wouldn't you say?"

"It sure is," said Mark. "Are those your dogs?"

"No," Chief Jackson answered. "Spot and Speckles live at the fire station. I'm walking them because they need some exercise."

"This is our dog, Woof," said Mark.

"Well, now," the fire chief said with a smile. "What kind of a dog is he? He doesn't look like a purebred."

"No, Woof ˙ just a mutt," said Mark, "but he's the smartest and best dog ... the world."

"I see," Chief Jackson replied, looking down at Woof's bent ear and crooked tail. He wasn't convinced.

"Have you put out any fires lately?" asked Mark.

"No," said the chief. "We've been lucky this summer. Everything has been pretty quiet."

Then his eyes brightened, and he said, "Hey, would you kids like to visit the station? We could show you around and teach you about fighting fires."

"Wow!" squealed Krissy. "We'd love it!"

"May we bring Woof?" asked Mark excitedly.

"Sure, bring him along," said the chief. "Come to my house Saturday morning, and I'll drive you to the station."

"Thanks!" said Mark.

Chief Jackson waved good-bye and walked away with the Dalmatians at his side.

"Come on. Let's tell Mom and Dad," said Krissy.

When Mr. and Mrs. Peterson heard the news, they were delighted.

"That sounds like a wonderful opportunity," said Father. "I know Chief Jackson very well. He has a great reputation in the city of Gladstone. Of course you may go."

When Saturday came, Mark and Krissy arrived at Chief Jackson's house. He met them at the door.

"Right on time," he said. "Let's be on our way, shall we?"

The children got in the front seat of Chief Jackson's pickup truck while Woof rode in the back. When they reached the fire station, both of the kids jumped out of the pickup and followed the chief. Woof was close behind.

Upon entering, Mark and Krissy looked around excitedly. There were so many interesting things going on.

Spot and Speckles were in the corner eating their breakfast, and several firemen were working on water hoses.

Some of the men were sliding down the pole from the room upstairs where their beds were. Others were polishing the two huge fire trucks parked in the garage. The firemen were making the red trucks shiny and beautiful.

When they saw their boss, they stopped working and said hello.

"Guys, I want you to meet some friends of mine," said the chief. "Say hello to Mark and Krissy Peterson and their dog, Woof."

The firemen smiled and said hi to the children.

"Andy will give you a tour while I get some coffee," said Chief Jackson.

The Peterson children shook hands with the fire chief's assistant.

"Would one of you like to sit behind the steering wheel of the biggest fire truck?" asked Andy.

"Wow! Would I!" exclaimed Mark, climbing onto the driver's seat. Mark felt so big and important sitting in the fire truck. There was a shiny chrome siren on top and lots of fancy radio equipment beneath the dashboard. On each side of the truck were tall ladders, and there was a big fire hose behind the backseat.

"Firemen can get to any house in the city in less than five minutes," said Andy. "It doesn't matter what time of day or night. We're always ready to go."

"Don't you ever sleep?" asked Krissy.

"Sure, but we take turns going to bed. If the fire bell rings, we're up, dressed, and down the pole in no time at all. That should help you kids to sleep better, just knowing we're always on duty."

"Mark, I want to get in the truck too," said Krissy. Just as she reached the front seat, a loud bell began to ring.

"Uh-oh!" said Andy. "We have an emergency. Get down, Krissy, Mark. We have to go."

The Peterson children climbed off the truck and backed out
of the way. Firemen began running in all directions, putting
on their coats and hats and jumping onto the truck. Chief
Jackson headed toward the front with Spot and Speckles.

"Stay here with Andy," he said to the children. "We'll be
back soon." Mark and Krissy watched as the big truck pulled
out of the driveway.

Suddenly Krissy gasped. "Oh no! Where's Woof?"

They turned in time to see a frightened Woof standing on the back of the fire engine as it sped away.

"There he goes!" yelled Krissy.

"What are we going to do?" asked Mark.

"Let's call Mom and Dad and see if they can help," she said.

Woof wasn't happy about his situation either. The loud siren hurt his ears, and he struggled to stay on his feet as the fire engine swayed around corners. Still, no one on the truck had noticed he was there.

Soon the firemen turned onto a side street and stopped in front of a burning house. They jumped off the truck and went to work. Some ran toward the house while others got the hoses ready to hook onto a nearby fire hydrant.

Spot and Speckles were waiting near the truck. They were trained to stay there so they would not be in the way.

Neighbors gathered around to watch the smoke and flames. Three firemen burst through the front door and ran into the house to make sure everyone was out. After finding no one inside, they quickly made a hole in the roof to let the smoke out. Then they ran outside to report that everyone was safe.

Just then one of the firemen saw two children crying. They were standing near the street with their parents.

"What's the matter?" he asked as he rushed over to them.

The children rubbed their eyes and looked up at the fireman's kind face.

"Our three puppies are trapped in the house," said the little girl. "The mother dog got out, but her babies are still inside."

"Is there anything you can do?" asked the boy anxiously.

The fireman frowned and shook his head. "I'm sorry," he said. "We can't risk someone's life to save them—the fire has become too dangerous for us to go back inside."

"But they're going to die!" the little girl sobbed.

"I'm sorry," said the fireman. "There's nothing we can do."

Just then Woof jumped off the truck and lifted his crooked ear! He had heard noises coming from the burning house! It was the sound of puppies yelping and whimpering.

Dogs can often hear what people can't, and Woof knew there was trouble in the house. Without wasting any time, he ran as fast as he could toward the front door. One of the firemen saw him dash into the house and yelled, "Stop!" But it was too late.

The Dalmatians danced and barked excitedly near the truck. They had heard the puppies' cries too, but they were afraid to go near the smoky house.

Inside, Woof crawled from room to room looking all
around. The smoke was so thick that he could hardly breathe!
It burned his eyes as he struggled to see where he was going.

Woof looked up and saw a heavy beam teetering above
him. He jumped back just before it came crashing down in
front of him.

He continued searching for the helpless puppies. Sometimes he had to crawl on his stomach to stay below the smoke. Woof followed the whines until he came to the kitchen. A burning cabinet fell near him with a crash, and dishes broke

on the floor. Still, Woof struggled to reach the frightened
puppies. He barked once to get their attention and continued
to crawl toward them, choking and coughing.

Meanwhile, Mark and Krissy arrived at the fire with their parents. They had seen the smoke high in the sky and had followed it to find the right location. The children jumped out of the car and ran to one of the firemen.

"Have you seen our dog?" asked Mark anxiously. "He has shaggy hair and a crooked tail, and he rode here on the fire truck by mistake."

"Yeah, I've seen the mutt. He ran into the house for some reason. I tried to stop him, but he kept right on going."

"Oh no!" cried Krissy. "Woof could die in there!"

"Why would he go into a burning house?" asked Mark. "Doesn't he know how dangerous it is?"

Woof knew about the danger, that's for sure! He was surrounded by fire and smoke!

By crawling on his belly, Woof was able to reach the puppies' bed. He grasped the smallest puppy by the loose skin on the back of its neck and carried it carefully in his mouth. The others whimpered and followed Woof toward the front door.

Exhausted, he staggered onto the porch. The puppy was
still dangling from his mouth, as the other two waddled out
behind him.

Mark and Krissy ran to their dog and threw their arms
around him. People in the crowd began cheering and
clapping.

A local newspaper reporter snapped Woof's picture, and the firemen were *very* impressed!

"You were right, Krissy and Mark," said Chief Jackson. "This *is* a very special dog!"

The mother dog licked Woof's face for saving her little ones, while the two children cuddled her pups. Woof was everyone's hero—the bravest and smartest dog of all!

The next day Mr. Peterson brought the Sunday paper in and placed it on the table. There on the front page was a picture of Woof holding a puppy in his mouth! Mark and Krissy squealed with delight when they saw the photo. The newspaper said he was "braver than the dogs that belonged to the fire station" and called him "Our Favorite Hero."

"Wasn't that an unselfish thing Woof did?" asked Krissy, reaching down to pat him on the head.

"It certainly was," said Father. "Woof cared more about saving the lives of the puppies than about his own safety. He might even have died for them."

Suddenly Mark thought of a Scripture he had memorized in Sunday school. "In John 15:13 Jesus said, 'Greater love has no one than this, that he lay down his life for his friends.'"

215

"That Scripture does have special meaning for us," said Father. "Woof was willing to die for his little friends. But there's a better example of a much greater act of love. It has to do with our heavenly Father loving us so much that he sent his only Son to die for us on the cross. That was the most wonderful thing ever done for people. Jesus died for all of his friends—that includes you and me!"

Just then the telephone rang. Mark answered it.

"Mark, this is Chief Jackson. All the men on the squad want to hang Woof's picture on the wall, and we'd like you to bring him down to receive an honorary medal."

"Thank you!" said Mark.

"Oh, one other thing," said the chief. "We'd like to adopt Woof and make him our main fire dog. Do you think he'd like that?"

"Well," said Mark, "that's a big honor, but Woof is happy just being a good ol' family dog. I think he'd like to stay here with us."

Chief Jackson chuckled and said, "I understand."

When Mark hung up the phone, he told the rest of the family about the chief's request.

"Dad, do you think Woof would rather belong to the firemen?" asked Mark.

Mr. Peterson smiled. "Why don't you ask *him?*"

Mark knelt by his dog and repeated the question. As if understanding every word, Woof suddenly knocked Mark and Krissy over and licked their faces.

"I think you have your answer," Mr. Peterson laughed.

WOOF AND THE BIG FIRE
Theme: Love unselfishly.

Talking about Woof

Why did Woof run into the burning house? Was it a difficult thing for him to do?

How did everyone treat Woof after the rescue?

Talking about Mark and Krissy

What did Krissy mean when she said that Woof did an unselfish thing?

Who did that remind Mark of?

Talking about Me

Can you think of any unselfish things you have done? What unselfish things have others done for you?

What is the most loving thing Jesus did for you?

Reading What the Bible Says

Greater love has no one than this, that he lay down his life for his friends.
John 15:13

Talking to God

Dear God, I'm really thankful for the love that your Son, Jesus, showed for me on the cross. Please help me remember to show unselfish love toward my family and friends.

    I want to pray for . . .
    Thank you for . . .
    I love you, God. In Jesus' name. Amen.

WOOF

THE
SEEING EYE DOG

THEME

Don't be proud.

Proverbs 16:18

It was just another day for Woof. A month before, he had rescued three puppies from a burning house and won the hearts of the whole town of Gladstone. He had been named "Our Favorite Hero" by the local newspaper, and his picture was on display at the fire department. All of this attention had caused Woof to feel pretty proud of himself—a little *too* proud. In fact, he was becoming impossible to live with.

Woof still loved the Peterson family—especially the children, Mark and Krissy. But he had begun to believe he didn't have to obey them. After all, a town hero shouldn't have to take orders from anyone!

Mark and Krissy first noticed the change when Woof refused to come when he was called. Sometimes he would even yawn and look the other way. This was not at all like the Woof they knew and loved.

Then there was the problem with his dog food. He refused to eat it! Woof felt he deserved ground hamburger, or maybe T-bone steaks—certainly more than the ordinary doggie crunchies in his bowl. After all, shouldn't the town hero eat better food than what "common" dogs are served?

Woof had definitely changed. Just yesterday he had done something completely forbidden at the Peterson home. When the family wasn't looking, Woof jumped onto the bed and slept on the pillows. He knew it was wrong, but he thought he was worth it.

Today Woof was stretched out in the sun, pretending he didn't hear Mark call his name. "Wow!" said ten-year-old Krissy. "Woof is really grouchy these days! He has never acted this way before."

"I know," agreed Mark, shutting the back door. "Ever since he became a hero, he hasn't been the same."

"Mom thinks Woof is too proud of himself," said Krissy. "He really believes he is better than everybody else."

"Remember what we learned last Sunday?" asked six-year-old Mark. "The Bible says that if we're proud, someday we'll fall. My Sunday school teacher said it means that when you are too proud, you sometimes get hurt. Pride makes you do bad things, and then you have to suffer for it."

Woof turned over on his back and rolled around on the grass. Then he yawned and thought about being the town hero.

227

Just then Scruffy came by for a visit. He was the tiny mutt that lived in the next block. The two dogs had been friends for years, but now Woof didn't want Scruffy around. The "town hero" rudely growled and chased his old friend from the yard. Woof didn't think Scruffy was good enough to be friends with him anymore. As Scruffy ran down the street, Woof barked twice to tell him not to come back.

"Did you see that?" Mark asked.

"Yeah!" said Krissy. "That was a mean thing to do. I think Mom is right about Woof."

Woof *did* feel a little guilty for the way he had treated his old pal. But then he forgot about it. After all, he had the right to run Scruffy away. He needed a new set of friends now that he was the "big dog" in town.

It wasn't long before Woof became bored in the backyard. Someone had left the gate open, so Woof decided to go for a stroll down Maple Street. He knew he wasn't supposed to leave the yard, but he decided one short trip around the block wouldn't hurt.

Proudly Woof trotted down the sidewalk, stopping every few seconds to sniff at a bush or a tree. He was so busy that he barely noticed who was coming from the other direction.

Suddenly Woof looked up in surprise! A beautiful German shepherd was walking toward him, leading Miss Richards down the street. She was blind and depended totally on her dog, Major, to help her get around.

Woof had never seen such a wonderful dog! The shepherd looked confident and acted well trained. He was big and powerful, too. Why, he could have bitten Woof in half if he had wanted!

Besides all of that, the German shepherd was also a beautiful purebred. He was very different from Woof, who was just an ordinary mutt. No one even knew who Woof's mother and father were. He stood silently as the shepherd walked by with his chest out and his head held high.

Just then a car rounded the corner and ran through a big puddle in the road. Before Woof could jump out of the way, the car splashed mud all over him.

Suddenly Woof felt ugly and foolish. He looked at his own crooked leg and tail. He thought about his bent ear and his rough, shaggy fur covered with mud.

Woof wished that he looked like the German shepherd. And he wished that he could help someone who was blind like Miss Richards. That was important work.

Woof felt terrible as he walked home with his tail between his legs.

When Mark and Krissy saw him slinking back, they scolded him for leaving the yard. Then they laughed out loud.

"You look *so* funny, Woof!" said Krissy.

"Yeah! You don't look so proud now," added Mark.

That night Woof couldn't stop thinking about the shepherd. The more he compared himself to that dog, the more ugly and worthless he felt. He finally went to sleep feeling very sad.

Father went back inside the house to tell Mother and the children the news.

"Wow!" shouted Mark. "Woof, the Seeing Eye dog!"

"That's right," said Father. "I think Woof can handle the job just fine. And it would only be until Major gets well."

Mark patted his dog on the head. "You're going to have to work hard to learn this important job," he said. "But I think you can do it."

Woof didn't understand all their words, but he knew the family was saying something important about him.

That night the Petersons and their dog arrived at Miss
Richards' house. Woof knew she was the lady he had seen
walking with the German shepherd. He also noticed that the
beautiful dog was not there.

Mr. Peterson hooked a harness around Woof's back, and
Woof quickly understood what he was being asked to do. He
was supposed to fill in for Major, the Seeing Eye dog!

238

The next day Woof began working with a trainer. He practiced walking up and down the sidewalk while the Peterson family watched from their living room.

At the end of the week Miss Richards knocked on the Petersons' front door. "You have a fine dog," she said, reaching down to pat his head. "The trainer thinks he is ready to take me to the supermarket."

The Petersons waved good-bye as Woof and Miss Richards headed down the street. Woof was feeling nervous as he led the way since he knew he was not as well trained as Major.

Once he stepped off a curb too soon, and the driver of an oncoming car had to slam on the brakes. Luckily neither Woof nor Miss Richards was hurt.

Another time he stopped to sniff at a trash can and almost made Miss Richards trip and fall. But she didn't seem to mind. She continued to praise him and tell him what a good dog he was. By the time they got to the supermarket, Woof was doing his job almost as well as Major.

When Woof and Miss Richards entered the grocery store, he couldn't believe that no one scolded him or asked him to leave. Whenever he went to town with Mark and Krissy, he always had to wait outside buildings for them to come out. After all, only Seeing Eye dogs are allowed in public places. This was the first time Woof had ever been inside a grocery store, and he was excited.

Woof enjoyed all the wonderful smells around him. The meat section nearly drove him crazy!

Slowly he led Miss Richards up and down the aisles. Even though she was blind, she could recognize foods by the way they felt or smelled. She loaded her shopping cart with eggs, milk, and butter, among other things.

Finally they came to the produce section. Miss Richards set her purse down on the fruit stand while she chose ripe oranges and apples.

Suddenly, out of the corner of his eye, Woof saw someone move! Coming toward them were the Harper twins—those mean, troublemaking brothers, Billy and Bobby, who lived next door to the Petersons. The boys had seen the purse on the fruit stand and were waiting to grab it. Miss Richards couldn't see the boys sneaking around the tomato bin, but Woof knew exactly what they were up to!

He stiffened his legs, and the hair stood up on the back of his neck.

"What's the matter, Woof?" asked Miss Richards, sensing that something was wrong.

Just then Bobby grabbed the purse. Woof lowered his head and growled angrily. A dog's growl does not have human words, but the boys understood what it meant. It said, "Don't you dare take that purse!"

The Harper twins looked at each other nervously because they knew Woof could be tough when he wanted. They began backing away from the dog. But before they could get away, Woof lunged toward the boys. He scared them so badly that Bobby dropped the purse, and both boys ran right into a bin of tomatoes. What a mess! Tomatoes flew in all directions, splattering on the floor and rolling down the aisle.

In their hurry to escape, Billy and Bobby Harper slipped on the tomatoes and slid across the floor! By the time they got to the exit, their shoes, pants, and even their faces were covered with smashed tomatoes. Woof watched with a doggie smile as the Harper twins ran from the supermarket.

After the store manager told Miss Richards what had happened, she patted Woof on the head. "Thanks for taking care of my purse, Woof," she said. "You're a wonderful friend!"

When they got home from the supermarket, Miss Richards telephoned the Petersons to tell them the story.

"Woof is a very special dog," she said. "I can see why you love him so much."

247

For the rest of the week, Woof took good care of Miss
Richards. She fed him ground hamburger as a special treat
and brushed his rough fur every day. She also gave him a
nice bed to sleep in each night.

Woof missed Mark and Krissy, but he knew how important
his job was to Miss Richards. It also made him feel good to do
something like Major, the German shepherd. However, this
time Woof didn't feel better than everyone else. He just felt
good about being able to help someone.

Finally Major came home from the animal hospital, and Woof went home to the Petersons. Mark and Krissy saw a big difference in the way he acted as soon as he returned. He came to them when he was called and ate all his doggie crunchies. He even brought Mr. Peterson his slippers. He became a good ol' dog again, and the family was happy to see the change.

"Woof doesn't seem too proud anymore," said Krissy.

"I think he's happy because he helped someone who needed him," Mark commented.

"That always makes us feel good about ourselves," said Father. "It doesn't really matter how we look or what our jobs are—what's important is how we treat others!"

The next day Woof invited Scruffy over to play chase. The two of them rolled in the grass, napped in the shade, and ate crunchies from the same dish. Oh, Woof was still a proud dog. But now he was proud to have a friend like Scruffy. And he was proud to be a member of the Peterson family, where everybody felt loved.

WOOF, THE SEEING EYE DOG
Theme: Don't be proud.

Talking about Woof

What was Woof's attitude at the beginning of the story?

What caused Woof to learn that his attitude was wrong?

Talking about Mark and Krissy

At the end of the story, what were some ways Mark and Krissy saw that Woof had changed?

What did Mark and Krissy think was the reason why Woof finally gave up his pride?

Talking about Me

How do you act when you are proud? Do people like to be around you then?

What kinds of things can you do for other people so you'll feel good about yourself without being proud?

Reading What the Bible Says

Pride goes before destruction, and haughtiness before a fall.
Proverbs 16:18

Talking to God

Dear God, teach me to put others first and not think too highly of myself. Help me not to be proud but to be thankful for the things you show me how to do.

> I want to pray for . . .
> Thank you for . . .
> I love you, God. In Jesus' name. Amen.

ABOUT THE AUTHOR

DANAE DOBSON, daughter of Dr. and Mrs. James Dobson, received a bachelor of arts degree in communication from Azusa Pacific University. She has written nineteen books for children, including *Parables for Kids,* which she coauthored with her father.

Writing has interested Danae since she was a young girl. She was only twelve years old when her first book about Woof was published! Her desire to help teach and inspire children is something she considers a top priority.

Danae appreciates the opportunities she has to visit her parents in Colorado. She also enjoys her church family and her friends—including their children!